# THE RED PAVILION

Judge Dee, the bearded detective of ancient China,
was only passing through Paradise Island on his way
home from the capital when the local magistrate, his old
friend Lo, asked him to wind up a suicide case for him.
'A mere matter of routine', his genial colleague calls
it—before he himself beats a hasty retreat from the
notorious island amusement resort, thriving on gambling,
prostitution and debauchery. Left to deal with the baffling situation, the judge is at once involved in the promis-
cuous love life of a beautiful courtesan, has to deal with
rape and murder, and gets enmeshed in a gruesome old
crime, committed thirty years before.

The Red Pavilion, where the chosen beauty-queens of
Paradise Island used to disport themselves with their
lucky lovers, has been the scene of three mysterious
deaths, including a murder in a sealed room. As Judge
Dee tackles these three complicated problems, he is
assisted by his lieutenant, the boxer Ma Joong, whose
amorous disposition again leads him into curious
adventures.

D0249453

Judge Dee Mysteries Available from Chicago:

# THE RED PAVILION

*A Judge Dee Mystery*

by

ROBERT VAN GULIK

*With six illustrations
drawn by the author in Chinese style*

# THE UNIVERSITY OF CHICAGO PRESS

The University of Chicago Press, Chicago 60637

Copyright © 1961 by Robert van Gulik

All rights reserved. Originally published 1961
University of Chicago Press Edition 1994
Printed in the United States of America
01 00 99 98 97 96 95 94        6 5 4 3 2 1


ISBN 0-226-84873-6 (pbk.)

**Library of Congress Cataloging-in-Publication Data**

Gulik, Robert Hans van, 1910–1967.
    The Red Pavilion / by Robert van Gulik, with six
    illustrations drawn by the author in Chinese style. —
    University of Chicago Press ed.
        p.   cm. — (A Judge Dee mystery)
    1.  Dee Jen-Djieh (Fictitious character)   2.  Detective
    and mystery stories, English.     3.  China—Fiction.
    I.  Title.   II.  Series: Gulik, Robert Hans van,
    1910–1967. Judge Dee mystery.
    PR9130.9.G8R4   1994
    823′.914—dc20                                    94-645
                                                       CIP

This book is printed on acid-free paper.

suddenly checked himself. He looked with dismay at the tall woman of commanding mien who had appeared in the door opening.

She was clad in a gorgeous robe of violet brocade, with a golden pattern of birds and flowers, a high collar and long, trailing sleeves. The broad purple sash, wound tight round her middle, showed to advantage her slender waist and generous bosom. Her hair was done up in a high chignon, bristling with long golden hairpins with jewelled knobs. Her smooth oval face was carefully powdered and rouged, and from her delicate small ears hung long pendants of carved green jade.

Feng bade her a boisterous welcome. She made a perfunctory bow, then quickly surveyed the table and asked him with a frown:

'Has Magistrate Lo not yet arrived?'

Feng hurriedly explained to her that the magistrate had to leave the island unexpectedly, but that His Excellency Dee, the magistrate of the neighbour district, was deputizing for him. He invited her to sit down on the chair next to the judge. Since she was there, Judge Dee thought he might as well get on good terms with her, and gather some information about the dead Academician. So he said cheerfully:

'Now we have been formally introduced! I am really in luck today!'

Autumn Moon gave him a cold stare. 'Fill my cup!' she snapped at Silver Fairy. As the plump girl hastily obeyed, the Queen Flower emptied it in one long draught, and had it refilled at once. Then she casually asked the judge:

'Didn't Magistrate Lo give you a message for me?'

'He charged me with conveying his sincere apologies to the present company,' Judge Dee answered, somewhat astonished. 'That doubtless also included you.'

She made no reply, but silently regarded her winecup for a while, her beautiful eyebrows creased in a deep frown. The judge noticed that the four others were eyeing her anxiously.

27

Suddenly she lifted her head and shouted at the two musicians:

'Don't sit there looking stupid, you two! Play something, that's what you are here for!'

As the two frightened girls began to play, the Queen Flower emptied her cup, again in one draught. Curiously observing his beautiful neighbour, Judge Dee noticed that the cruel lines about her mouth had deepened; she was evidently in a vile temper. She looked up and darted a searching look at Feng. He averted his eyes and quickly began a conversation with Tao Pan-te.

Suddenly the judge understood. On the veranda she had told him that she was to become the wife of a magistrate who was also a poet, and wealthy. And Lo was a poet, and said to have ample private means! Amusedly he reflected that evidently it was his amorous colleague who, during the investigation of the suicide, had become involved with the Queen Flower, and in an unguarded moment had rashly promised to redeem and marry her. That explained his precipitate, nearly stealthy departure. Urgent official business, forsooth! The genial magistrate must soon have discovered that he had chosen for playmate an ambitious and ruthless woman, who would not hesitate to put pressure on him, utilizing the fact that he had allowed himself to become intimate with an important witness in a court-case. No wonder he was eager to leave the island! But the confounded fool had left him, his colleague, in a most embarrassing position. Of course Feng and the others knew all about Lo's infatuation, and therefore had invited Autumn Moon. Probably the dinner was even meant to celebrate Magistrate Lo's buying the girl out! Hence their consternation when they realized that Lo had taken to his heels. They must have understood also that Lo had thrown dust in his eyes, they must take him, solemnly created an Assessor, for an incredible fool! Well, he must try to brazen it out.

He bestowed an amiable smile on the courtesan and said:

'Just now I heard that it was the famous Academician Lee

Lien who killed himself because of you. How truly the Ancients observed that talented and handsome young men always fall in love with talented and beautiful women!'

Autumn Moon gave him a sidelong glance. She said, more friendly now:

'Thank you for the compliment. Yes, Lee was a charming fellow, in his own way. He gave me a vial of perfume as a parting present, in an envelope on which he had written a rather sweet poem. Came over to my pavilion specially to present it to me, on the very night the poor man did away with himself. He knew I like expensive scents!' She sighed, then went on pensively: 'I should have encouraged him a bit, after all. He was very considerate, and generous too. I didn't get round yet to opening the envelope, I wonder what perfume it is! He knew I like musk, or Indian sandal essence. I asked him about it when he was taking his leave, but he wouldn't tell me, just said: "See that it reaches its destination!"—meaning me! He would have his little jokes! What perfume do you think goes best with my type, sandal or musk?'

Judge Dee started on an elaborate compliment, but he was interrupted by the sounds of a scuffle on the other side of the table. Silver Fairy, who was filling the old curio-dealer's beaker, now made a frantic attempt to push his hands away from her bosom. The wine spilled on his robe.

'You clumsy fool!' Autumn Moon shouted at her. 'Can't you be more careful? And your hair-do is all awry! Go at once to the dressing-room and fix yourself up!'

The Queen Flower eyed the frightened girl speculatively as she scurried to the door. Turning to the judge, she asked coyly:

'Wouldn't you pour me some wine? As a special favour?'

Filling her cup, he noticed that she was looking flushed, the strong wine seemed to be having some effect on her at last. She moistened her lips with the tip of her tongue and smiled softly, her thoughts apparently elsewhere. After she had taken a few sips she suddenly rose, and said: 'I beg to be excused, I'll be back presently!'

After she had gone the judge tried to engage Kia Yu-po in a conversation, but the young poet had relapsed in his morose mood. New dishes were brought in, and all ate with gusto. The two musicians played several fashionable tunes. Judge Dee did not like the new-fangled music, but he had to admit that the food was delicious.

When the last fish course was being served, Autumn Moon came back, apparently in high spirits. While passing behind the curio-dealer she whispered something into his ear, then went on, after playfully tapping his shoulder with her fan. Sitting down, she said to the judge:

'This is turning out to be a most pleasurable evening after all!' She laid her hand on his arm, bent her head so close that he could smell the musk perfume in her hair, and said softly: 'Shall I tell you why I was so curt when we met on the veranda? Because I hated to admit to myself that I liked you. At first sight!' She gave him a long look, then went on: 'And you didn't dislike me either, did you—as you saw me?'

While Judge Dee was still groping for a suitable reply she squeezed his arm, and resumed quickly:

'It's so nice to meet a wise and experienced man like you! You don't know how utterly those so-called modern, young whippersnappers bore me! It's such a relief to meet a mature man like you, who . . .' She gave him a shy look, then lowered her eyes and added very softly: 'Who knows about . . . things.'

The judge saw with relief that Wen Yuan had got up from his chair and was preparing to take his leave. He said that an important client was coming to see him after dinner, and asked politely to be excused.

The Queen Flower now began to exchange jokes with Feng and Tao. Although she drank many more cups in quick succession, her speech didn't become slurred, and her retorts were witty and to the point. But at last, after Feng had told a funny

30

story, she suddenly put her hand to her forehead and said plaintively:

'Oh, I have drunk too much! Would you gentlemen think it very rude if I retired now? This is my parting cup!'

She took up Judge Dee's own wine beaker and slowly drank it. Then she bowed and left.

As the judge was staring with disgust at the red smear of lipsalve on the rim of his beaker, Tao Pan-te remarked, with a thin smile:

'You have made a great impression on our Queen Flower, sir!'

'She only wanted to be polite to a stranger,' Judge Dee said deprecatingly.

Kia Yu-po rose and asked to be excused, he said he didn't feel very well. The judge realized with dismay that he himself couldn't leave before another long interval had elapsed, for if he went too soon the others would think he was going after the courtesan. Her drinking from his beaker had been an unequivocal invitation. What a situation that scoundrel Lo had landed him in! With a sigh he started on the sweet soup that marked the approaching end of the dinner.

## IV

After Ma Joong had parted from Judge Dee at the gate of the Crane Bower, he walked down the street, whistling a gay tune. Soon he found the main thoroughfare of the island.

People of all descriptions were milling around under the ornamental arches of coloured stucco that spanned the street at regular intervals, and elbowing their way in and out of the high gates of the gambling halls. Vendors of cakes and noodles had to shout at the top of their voices to make themselves heard in this noisy crowd. Every time the din lessened somewhat one heard the clanking of copper coins, shaken in a large wooden trough by a pair of sturdy fellows, at the entrance of each gambling hall. They keep at it all night long, for this auspicious sound of money is supposed to bring good luck, and it also attracts customers.

Ma Joong halted before a high wooden platform, put up next to the door of the largest gambling hall. It was loaded with piles of platters and bowls, filled with sweetmeats and candied fruit. Over it was a scaffolding that carried rows of paper models, representing houses, chariots, boats, all sorts of furniture, and piles of folded clothes, also made of paper. This was one of the many altars put up at the beginning of the seventh month, for the benefit of the souls of the departed that roam about freely among the living, all during the Festival of the Dead. The ghosts may taste from the food, and choose from the paper models what they need for their life in the Hereafter. On the thirtieth of the seventh month, at the close of the festival, the food is distributed among the poor, and the altars and the paper models are burned, the smoke carrying the chosen objects to their unearthly destination. The festival reminds the people that death is not a final parting, for once every year the departed come back and for a few weeks take part in the lives of those who had been dear to them.

After Ma Joong had admired the display, he said to himself with a grin:

'Uncle Peng's soul won't be here! He didn't have much of a sweet tooth, but he was mighty fond of a round of gambling, in his day! Must have been lucky at it too, seeing that he left me two good, solid gold bars! I bet his soul is floating about over the gaming tables. I'd better go inside, maybe he'll give his young nephew a few useful tips!'

He entered the hall, paid ten coppers, and watched for a while the dense crowd round the large gaming table in the centre. Here the simplest and most popular game was in progress, one had to bet on the exact number of copper coins that the superintendent of the table covered under an upturned rice bowl. Then he elbowed his way to the staircase in the back.

In the large room upstairs the gamblers were seated in groups of six round a dozen or so smaller tables, engaged in various games with cards and dice. Here all the customers were well-dressed, at one table Ma Joong noticed two men wearing official caps. On the back wall hung a red signboard, inscribed in large black letters: 'Every game must be settled at once and in cash.'

While Ma Joong was debating with himself what table he should join, a small hunchback sidled up to him. He wore a neat blue dress but his large head with the tousled grey hair was bare. Looking up at Ma Joong's towering figure with his beady eyes, he said in a shrill voice:

'If you want a game, you'll have to show me how much cash you carry.'

'What has that got to do with you?' Ma Joong asked angrily.

'Everything!' a deep voice spoke up behind him.

Ma Joong turned round and found himself face to face with an enormous man, as tall as himself but with a chest as round

33

as a barrel. His large head seemed to grow directly from his broad shoulders and his breast was bulging like the shell of a crab. He gave Ma Joong a searching look from his round, slightly protruding eyes.

'Who might you be?' Ma Joong asked, astonished.

'I am the Crab,' the large man explained in a tired voice. 'My colleague here is called the Shrimp. At your service.'

'Haven't you also got a fellow called Salt?' Ma Joong asked.

'No. Why?'

'So that I can mash you all three together in boiling water and have myself a meal,' Ma Joong replied contemptuously.

'Tickle me, will you?' the Crab asked the hunchback sadly. 'I am supposed to laugh at customers' jokes.'

The Shrimp ignored him. Looking up at Ma Joong along his thin, pointed nose, he asked sharply:

'Can't you read? The signboard over there says that customers have to settle in cash. To prevent disappointment on the part of all concerned, newcomers have to show us how much they can afford to stake.'

'That's not unreasonable,' Ma Joong agreed reluctantly. 'You two belong to this establishment?'

'Me and the Shrimp are observers,' the Crab said quietly. 'Employed by Mr Feng Dai, the warden.'

Ma Joong regarded the incongruous pair with a speculative eye. Then he reached down and pulled his official pass from his boot. Handing it to the Crab, he said:

'I work for Magistrate Dee of Poo-yang, who is now the Assessor in charge here. I'd like to have a quiet talk with you.'

The pair scrutinized the pass. The Crab gave it back to Ma Joong, saying with a sigh:

'That means a parched throat. Let's sit out on the balcony, Mr Ma, and have a drink and a snack. On the house.'

The three men sat down in a corner from where the Crab could keep an eye on the gamblers inside. Soon a waiter placed a large platter heaped with fried rice and three pewter wine-jugs on their table.

During the exchange of the usual polite inquiries it turned out that the Crab and the Shrimp had lived all their lives on Paradise Island. The Crab was a boxer of the eighth grade; soon he and Ma Joong were deep in a discussion on the merits of various blows and grips. The small hunchback did not take part in this technical conversation, he concentrated on the rice, which disappeared with amazing speed. When there was nothing left on the platter, Ma Joong took a long draught from his wine beaker, leaned back in his chair and said contentedly, patting his belly:

'Now that the preliminary work has been successfully completed, I feel strong enough for tackling official business. What do you fellows know about the Academician Lee?'

The Crab exchanged a quick look with the Shrimp. The latter said:

'So that's what your boss is after, eh? Well, to give you the gist, the Academician began and ended his stay here badly, but in between he had lots of fun, I understand.'

The sounds of an altercation came from the room. The Crab was up and inside with a speed amazing in so ponderous a man. The Shrimp emptied his wine cup and resumed:

'This is how it was. Ten days ago, on the eighteenth, the Academician and five friends arrive here, in a large boat, from the capital. They had spent two days on the river, and every day they had been drinking and feasting from morning till night. The boatmen had dutifully taken care of the left-overs, so all were drunk. There's a thick mist, their boat rams a junk belonging to our boss Feng, carrying his daughter. She was coming back from a visit to relatives in the village upstream, There's considerable damage, they don't reach the landing stage here till dawn, and the Academician has to promise to pay a round sum, in settlement of the damage. That's what I meant when I said that his stay on the island began badly, you see.

35

Then he and his friends go to the Hostel of Eternal Bliss, the Academician rents for himself the Red Pavilion.'

'That's the selfsame place my boss is staying in!' Ma Joong exclaimed. 'But he isn't afraid of ghosts. I suppose the Academician committed suicide right there?'

'I didn't mention suicides, neither did I mention ghosts,' the hunchback said pointedly.

The Crab, who was re-joining them, had heard the last remark.

'We don't talk gladly about ghosts,' he said, sitting down again. 'And the Academician didn't commit suicide.'

'Why?' Ma Joong asked, astonished.

'Because,' the Shrimp resumed, 'as an observer, I observed him. Here, at the gaming table. Remained cool as a cucumber, winning or losing. Not the suicide type. That's why.'

'We have been observing people here for ten years, you know,' the Crab added. 'Know all the types, every single one of them. Take that young poet, Mr Kia Yu-po. Lost all his money here, every last copper, in one sitting. The high-strung, excitable type. Might commit suicide as soon as you have turned your head. As to the Academician, no sir. No suicide for him. Never.'

'He became involved with a woman, though,' Ma Joong remarked. 'Women often make a man behave like a fool. When I think of the things they made me do, sometimes . . .'

'He didn't commit suicide,' the Crab repeated stolidly. 'He was a cold, calculating bastard. If a wench jilted him, he would try to play her a dirty trick. Not kill himself.'

'The alternative is murder!' Ma Joong said dryly.

The Crab looked shocked. He asked the Shrimp:

'I didn't mention the word murder, did I?'

'You didn't!' the hunchback replied firmly.

Ma Joong shrugged.

'Who was the wench he slept with?' he asked.

'He saw much of our Queen Flower during the week he

stayed here,' the Shrimp replied, 'but he also saw much of Carnation, of the next street, and of Jade Flower, and of Peony. He may have had with them what you law-officers call carnal relations, then again he may have only tickled them a bit, playful-like. Ask the girls, not me. I wasn't there to hold their legs.'

'Might be an interesting line of inquiry!' Ma Joong said with a grin. 'In any case, they had a good time, tickling or otherwise. Then what happened?'

'Three days ago, the morning of the twenty-fifth,' the Shrimp went on, 'the Academician rents a boat for his five friends, and sends them off, back to the capital. He returns to the Red Pavilion, takes his luncheon there, alone. He spends the afternoon in his room, for the first time he doesn't go to the tables. He dines alone, also for the first time. Then he locks himself in his room, and a few hours later is found with his throat cut.'

'Amen,' said the Crab.

The Shrimp pensively scratched his long nose. He resumed:

'Now most of this is based on hearsay, you know. Take it or leave it. With our own eyes we observed only this: the curio-dealer Wen Yuan went to that hostel that night, some time after dinner.'

'So he visited the Academician!' Ma Joong said eagerly.

'Those fellows of the tribunal do put words in one's mouth, don't they?' the hunchback asked the Crab plaintively.

'It's their habit!' the Crab replied with a shrug.

'I said, my friend,' the Shrimp explained patiently, 'that we observed Wen going to the hostel. That's all.'

'Heavens,' Ma Joong exclaimed, 'if, besides visitors from outside, you two keep an eye also on all your prominent citizens, you must have a busy life!'

'We don't keep an eye on all our prominent citizens,' the Crab said. 'Only on Wen.' The Shrimp nodded emphatically. 'Three trades bring in the big money here,' the Crab continued, looking earnestly at Ma Joong with his protruding eyes. 'One, gambling and whoring, that's our boss Feng's business. Two, eating and drinking, that's Mr Tao's business. Three, buying and selling antiques, that is the affair of Mr Wen. Stands to reason that the three trades keep in close contact. If a fellow wins much at the tables, we pass on the good word to Tao's and Wen's men. Maybe the fellow wants to throw a big party, maybe he'll want to invest his money in a beautiful antique—expertly faked. Contrariwise, if a fellow loses heavily, we'll see whether the man hasn't perhaps a good-looking concubine or maidservant to sell, and Wen's men'll approach him about any good antique he might want to dispose of. And so on. Work out all possible combinations for yourself.'

'Sound business organization!' Ma Joong remarked.

'Perfect,' the Shrimp agreed. 'Thus we have Feng, Tao and Wen. Our boss Feng is a straight, honest man, so the government appointed him warden of the island. That gives him a finger in every pie, and makes him the wealthiest of the three. But he has to work for it, mind you! If the warden is honest, everybody here makes good profits, and the customers are content. Only fools who ask for it get cheated. If the warden is crooked, profits increase twenty times, including his own. But then this place goes to the dogs in no time at all. Thus, it's fortunate that Feng is straight. But he has no son, only a daughter. So if he dies, or gets into trouble, the job goes to someone else. Tao Pan-te is a scholar-like gentleman, doesn't like meddling. He would never want to be warden. Now, you know about Feng and Tao, two prominent citizens. I didn't mention Wen Yuan, did I now, Crab?'

'You didn't!' the Crab said gravely.

'What do you mean by telling me all this?' Ma Joong asked crossly.

'He described a situation for you,' the Crab replied.

'Right!' the Shrimp said with satisfaction. 'I described a situation, as I observed it. But, inasmuch as you seem a good fellow, Mr Ma, I'll add something I only have from hearsay. Thirty years ago Tao's father, a gentleman called Tao Kwang, committed suicide in the Red Pavilion. Window barred, door locked on the inside. And thirty years ago, on that selfsame night, the curio-dealer Wen was also seen near the hostel. Call it a coincidence.'

'Well,' Ma Joong said cheerfully, 'I'll tell my boss that he'll have to reckon with two ghosts in his bedroom. Now that we have dealt with the official business, I want your advice on a purely personal problem.'

The Crab sighed. He said wearily to the Shrimp:

'He wants a wench.' And, to Ma Joong: 'Heavens, man, walk into any house you like in the next street. You'll find all types, all special skills, all sizes. Just help yourself!'

'Precisely because you have such a varied stock here,' Ma Joong explained, 'I want something extra-special. I am a native of Foo-ling in this province, and tonight I want a girl from there.'

The Crab rolled up his round eyes.

'Hold my hand!' he told the Shrimp disgustedly. 'I am going to burst out in tears. A girl from his own village!'

'Well,' Ma Joong said, somewhat self-consciously, 'it just so happens that I haven't made love in my own dialect for quite a few years.'

'He's a sleep-talker. Bad habit,' the Crab commented to the Shrimp. He went on to Ma Joong: 'All right. Go to the Blue Tower, in the south quarter. Tell the woman in charge we want her to reserve Silver Fairy for you. She's from Foo-ling, superior quality above and below the navel, and a friendly person. She also sings well, being taught by a Miss Ling, in the olden days a famous courtesan here. But you won't be interested in music, I suppose. Go to the Blue Tower towards midnight, now it's too early, she'll be out attending a dinner somewhere. Then you do your talking tricks. Need our advice on that too?'

'Not yet! Anyway, thanks for the tip. You sound as if you don't care much for women, though.'

'We don't,' the Shrimp said. 'Does a baker eat his own pastries?'

'Well, not every day, probably,' Ma Joong admitted. 'But now and then he'll take a bite, I suppose. Just to see whether his stock hasn't gone stale on him. Without the skirts life'd be a bit boring, I'd say.'

'There's pumpkins,' the Crab observed gravely.

'Pumpkins?' Ma Joong exclaimed.

The Crab nodded ponderously. He took a toothpick from the lapel of his robe and started to work his teeth.

'We grow them,' the Shrimp explained. 'The Crab and me own a small house on the riverbank, over on the west side of the island. We have a nice patch of land; there we grow pumpkins. We come home from our work at dawn, water the pumpkins, then go to sleep. We wake up late in the afternoon, we weed the patch, water it again; then we come back here.'

'Everybody his own taste! Seems a bit monotonous to me, though.'

'You are wrong,' the Crab said earnestly. 'You should watch them grow! There are no two pumpkins alike. Never.'

'Tell him about us watering the pumpkins ten days ago,' the Shrimp said casually. 'The morning we found caterpillars on the leaves.'

The Crab nodded. He studied his toothpick, then said:

'The same morning we saw the Academician's boat arriving at the landing stage, that was. Quay is right opposite our pumpkin patch, you know. Wen, the curio-dealer, had a long talk with the Academician there. Stealthy-like, behind the trees. Now the Academician's father used to buy a lot from Wen, so his son knows him. Only I don't think they talked about antiques, by the looks of it, at least. We never leave off observing, you see. Even in our own time, and even when there are caterpillars threatening our pumpkins.'

'We are loyal servants of Mr Feng,' the Shrimp added. 'We have eaten his rice these last ten years.'

The Crab threw his toothpick away and got up.

'Now Mr Ma wants a game,' he said. 'Which brings us back to where we started. How much can you afford to spend, Mr Ma?'

# V

Ma Joong played a number of rounds with three solemn rice merchants. He got fairly good cards, but didn't enjoy himself. He liked a boisterous game, with lusty shouting and hearty cursing. First he won a little, then lost it again. That seemed a good moment to leave, so he got up from the table, said goodbye to the Crab and the Shrimp, and sauntered back to the Crane Bower.

The manager informed him that warden Feng's dinner was nearing its end, two of the guests and the courtesans had left already. He invited him to sit down on the bench next to the counter and have a cup of tea.

Soon he saw Judge Dee coming down the broad staircase, accompanied by Feng Dai and Tao Pan-te. While the two men were conducting him to his palankeen, the judge said to Feng:

'Tomorrow morning I'll come to your office directly after breakfast for the formal court session. See to it that all papers regarding the Academician's suicide are ready for me. I also want your coroner to be there.'

Ma Joong helped the judge to ascend the palankeen.

While they were being carried along, Judge Dee told his lieutenant what he had learned about the suicide. He discreetly omitted his discovery of Magistrate Lo's infatuation, confining himself to the remark that his colleague had been right in calling the suicide a routine matter.

'Feng's men don't share that view, sir,' Ma Joong said soberly. He reported in detail what the Crab and the Shrimp had told him. When he had finished, the judge said impatiently:

'Your friends are wrong. Didn't I tell you that the door was locked on the inside? And you saw the barred window. No one could get in through there.'

'But isn't it a curious coincidence, sir, that when Tao's father committed suicide in that same room thirty years ago, the old curio-dealer was seen there too?'

'Your two aquatic friends let themselves be carried away by their resentment against Wen, the rival of their boss Feng. They evidently want to cause trouble for the curio-dealer. I met him tonight, he is indeed a nasty old man. I wouldn't put it beyond him to scheme against Feng and try to replace him as warden of Paradise Island. But murder is quite a different proposition! And why should Wen want to murder the Academician, the very man whose help he was enlisting for ousting Feng? No, my friend, your two informants were contradicting themselves. And let's not get mixed up in these local bickerings.' He thought for a while, pensively pulling at his moustache. Then he resumed: 'What Feng's two men told you about the Academician's activities during his stay here nicely completes the picture. I met the woman he killed himself for. Met her twice, worse luck!'

After he had related the conversation on the veranda of the Red Pavilion, he added:

'The Academician may have been an able and learned scholar, but he can't have been a good judge of women. Although the Queen Flower is indeed a striking beauty, at heart she is a callous, fickle creature. Fortunately she attended only the second half of the dinner. The food was excellent, I must say, and I had an interesting conversation with Tao Pan-te, and with a young poet called Kia Yu-po.'

'That is the unlucky fellow who lost all his money at the tables!' Ma Joong remarked. 'And in one sitting, too!'

Judge Dee raised his eyebrows.

'That's odd! Feng told me that Kia will soon marry his only daughter!'

'Well, that's one way for a man to get his lost money back!' Ma Joong said with a grin.

Their palankeen was set down in front of the Hostel of

Eternal Bliss. Ma Joong picked a candle up at the counter, then they crossed the courtyard and walked through the garden to the dark corridor leading to the Red Pavilion.

Judge Dee opened the carved door of the antechamber. Suddenly he stood stock-still. Pointing at the ray of light that came from under the door of the Red Room on the left, he said in a low voice:

'That's strange! I distinctly remember that I doused the candles before leaving.' He stooped, then added: 'And the key I left in the lock has gone.'

Ma Joong pressed his ear to the door.

'Can't hear anything! Shall I knock?'

'Let's first have a look through the window.'

They quickly went through the sitting-room out on to the veranda, and tiptoed to the barred window. Ma Joong uttered an oath.

On the red carpet, in front of the bedstead, lay a naked woman. She was flat on her back, legs and arms stretched out, her head turned away from them.

'Is she dead?' Ma Joong asked in a whisper.

'Her breast doesn't move.' The judge pressed his face to the iron bars. 'Look, the key is in the lock!'

'That makes it the third suicide in this accursed room!' Ma Joong exclaimed worriedly.

'I am not so sure it's suicide,' Judge Dee muttered. 'I think I see a blue bruise on the side of her neck. Go to the office and tell the manager to fetch Feng Dai, at once! Don't say anything about our discovery, though.'

When Ma Joong had rushed off, the judge peered inside again. The red curtains of the bedstead were drawn open, exactly as when he had left. But next to the pillow he saw a folded-up white garment. More woman's clothes were piled up on the nearest chair, also neatly folded. A pair of diminutive silk shoes were standing in front of the bedstead.

'The poor, conceited wench!' he said softly. 'She was very sure of herself! And now she is dead.'

He turned away from the window and sat down by the balustrade. Sounds of singing and laughter came drifting over from the house in the park, the party there was still in full swing. Only a few hours ago she had been standing there at the balustrade, flaunting her voluptuous body. She had been a vain and pretentious woman, yet one shouldn't judge her too harshly, he thought. The fault lay not with her alone. The exaggerated veneration for physical beauty, the cult of carnal love, and the hectic hankering after gold that prevail in such an amusement resort must spoil a woman, giving her a distorted view of all values. The queen of the island's flowers had been rather a pathetic person, after all.

He was roused from his musings by the arrival of Feng Dai. He came out on the veranda accompanied by Ma Joong, the manager, and two sturdy men.

'What happened, sir?' Feng asked excitedly.

Judge Dee pointed at the barred window. Feng and the manager stepped up to it. They shrank back with a gasp.

The judge rose.

'Tell your men to break the door open!' he ordered the warden.

In the antechamber Feng's two henchmen threw themselves against the door. When it didn't budge, Ma Joong joined their efforts. The wood round the lock splintered away and the door swung open.

'Stay where you are!' Judge Dee ordered. He stepped over the threshold and from there studied the prone figure. He couldn't see any wound or traces of blood on Autumn Moon's smooth white body. But she must have died in a terrible manner for he saw now that her face was horribly distorted, the glazed eyes were bulging from their sockets.

He went into the room and squatted down by the side of the dead woman. He placed his hand under her left breast. The

45

body was still warm, the heart must have ceased beating not so long ago. He closed the eye-lids, then examined her throat. On either side were blue bruises. Someone must have throttled her, but there were no marks of fingernails. He went over the perfect body. There were no other signs of violence, only a few long, thin scratches on her forearms. They looked quite recent, and he was certain those hadn't been there when he saw her practically naked on the veranda. He turned the corpse over, but the shapely back showed no marks of any kind. Finally, he scrutinized her hands. The long, carefully tended fingernails were intact. Under them he found only bits of fluff from the red carpet.

He rose and surveyed the room. There were no signs of a struggle. He motioned the others to come inside, and said to Feng Dai:

'It's clear what brought her here, after our dinner. Apparently she had expected to pass the night with me in order to start a liaison. She had been under the mistaken impression that Magistrate Lo would buy her out, and when she found she had been wrong, she decided that I might do as well. While she was waiting for me here, something happened. For the time being we'll call it accidental death, for as far as I can see nobody could have entered this room. Tell your men to remove the body to your office, for the autopsy. Tomorrow morning I shall deal with this case at the court session. Summon Wen Yuan, Tao Pan-te and Kia Yu-po to appear there too.'

When Feng had left, Judge Dee asked the manager:

'Did you or anyone else see her enter the hostel?'

'No, Your Honour. But there's a short-cut from her pavilion on the plot next to ours, leading to the veranda here.'

The judge went to the bedstead and looked up at the canopy. It was higher than usual. He tapped the wooden panels of the back wall, but found no hollow sound. He turned to the manager, who couldn't keep his eyes off the white corpse, and snapped:

'Don't stand there and goggle! Speak up, is there any secret peephole or other queer device in this bedstead?'

'Certainly not, sir!' He looked again at the dead woman, then stammered: 'First the Academician, now the Queen Flower, I . . . I can't understand what . . .'

'Neither can I!' the judge cut him short. 'What is on the other side of this room?'

'Nothing, Your Honour! That's to say, there's no other room. Only the outer wall, and our side garden.'

'Did queer things ever happen in this room before? Speak the truth!'

'Never, Your Excellency!' the manager wailed. 'I have been in charge here more than fifteen years, hundreds of guests have stayed here and I never heard any complaints. I don't know how . . .'

'Fetch me your register!'

The manager scurried away. Feng's men came in with a stretcher. They rolled the dead woman in a blanket and carried her away.

In the meantime the judge had searched the sleeves of the violet robe. He found nothing but the usual brocade folder with comb and tooth-pick, a package of Autumn Moon's visiting cards, and two handkerchiefs. Then the manager returned with a ledger under his arm. 'Put it on the table!' Judge Dee barked at him.

Left alone with Ma Joong, the judge went over to the table and sat down with a tired sigh.

His tall lieutenant took the tea-pot from its basket and poured out a cup for the judge. Pointing at the red smear on the rim of the other cup, he remarked casually:

'She had a cup of tea before she died. And alone, for the second cup I just filled was quite dry.'

The judge set the full cup down abruptly.

'Pour this tea back into the pot,' he said curtly. 'Tell the manager to get you a sick cat or dog, and let it drink it.'

After Ma Joong had gone, Judge Dee pulled the ledger towards him and began to leaf through it.

Sooner than he had expected Ma Joong came back. He shook his head.

'The tea was all right, sir.'

'That's bad! I thought that someone had perhaps accompanied her here, and put poison in the tea before he left her. And that she had drunk it after she had locked herself in. That was the only rational explanation of her death.'

He leaned back in his chair, disconsolately tugging at his beard.

'But what about the bruises on her throat, Your Honour?'

'Those were only superficial, and there were no nail marks on the skin, just blue spots. They might have been caused by some poison unknown to me, but certainly not by someone trying to throttle her.'

Ma Joong worriedly shook his large head. He asked uneasily:

'What could have happened to her, sir?'

'We have those long thin scratches on her arms. Of undetermined origin, just like those found on the arms of the Academician. His death and that of his mistress, both in this same Red Room, must be connected in some way or other. Strange affair! I don't like it at all, Ma Joong.' He thought for a while, caressing his sidewhiskers. Then he sat up straight and resumed: 'While you were away I carefully studied the entries here in this ledger. In the past two months about thirty people have been staying in the Red Pavilion for shorter or longer periods. Now most of the entries have in the margin a woman's name, and an additional sum of money, marked down in red ink. Do you know what that means?'

'That's simple! It means that those guests slept here with a professional girl. The amount marked indicates the commission those women had to pay to the hostel's management.'

'I see. Well, the Academician slept here on his first night, the 19th that is, with a girl called Peony. On the two following

48

nights with Jade Flower, and on those of the 22nd and 23rd with a woman called Carnation. He died on the night of the 25th.'

'That one wasted night got him!' Ma Joong said with a bleak smile.

The judge hadn't heard the remark. He went on pensively:

'Curious that Autumn Moon's name doesn't appear here.'

'There's always the afternoon! Some men take their tea in a rather elaborate fashion!'

Judge Dee closed the ledger. He let his gaze wander about the room. Then he got up and walked over to the window. After he had felt the thick iron bars and checked the solid wooden frame, he remarked:

'There's nothing wrong with this window, no human being could have entered the room through it. And we can rule out any other hocus-pocus with this window too, for she was lying more than ten feet away from it; she fell backwards facing the door, not the window. Her head was turned slightly to the left, towards the bedstead.' He shook his head dejectedly and resumed: 'You had better go now and have a good night's rest, Ma Joong. I want you to go to the landing stage tomorrow morning at dawn. Try to locate the captain of Feng Dai's junk, and let him tell you all about the collision of the two boats. Make also discreet inquiries about the meeting of the Academician and the curio-dealer that, according to your two pumpkin-raising friends, took place there. I'll examine that bedstead again, then go to sleep too. Tomorrow we'll have a busy day.'

'You aren't going to sleep here in this room, sir?' Ma Joong asked, aghast.

'Of course I will!' the judge said peevishly. 'That'll give me a chance to verify whether there's really something wrong here. You can go now and find yourself a lodging. Good night!'

Ma Joong thought a moment of protesting, but when he saw Judge Dee's determined expression he realized that it would be useless. He bowed and took his leave.

The judge stood himself in front of the bedstead, his hands clasped behind his back. He saw that the thin silk cover of the bedmat showed some creases. Feeling them with his forefinger, he found they were slightly damp. He stooped and smelled the pillow. There was the musk scent he had noticed in the courtesan's hair when she was sitting next to him during the dinner.

It was easy to reconstruct the first phase. She had entered the Red Pavilion by the veranda, probably after a brief visit to her own pavilion. She might have intended to wait for him in the sitting-room, but when she found that the key was left in the lock of the Red Room, she thought the meeting could be more effectively staged inside there. She had a cup of tea, then she took off her upper robe, folded it and laid it on the chair. After she had stripped naked, she placed her undergarment on the bedstead, next to the pillow. Sitting on the edge of the bed, she took off her shoes and put them neatly on the floor. Finally she laid herself down, waiting till she would hear him knock. She must have lain there for quite some time, her perspiring back had creased the silk cover. He couldn't even guess at what happened next. Something must have occurred that made her leave the bed, and very calmly. For if she had jumped off in a hurry, the pillow and the cover would have been disturbed. As soon as she was standing in front of the bedstead, a terrible thing happened. He suddenly shivered when he recalled the expression of utter horror on the woman's contorted face.

He pushed the pillow aside and drew the silk cover away. Underneath was nothing but the bedmat of closely woven, soft reed, and under it solid wooden boards. He went to the table and took the candle. He found that, by standing on the bed, he could just reach the canopy. He tapped it with his knuckles but heard no hollow sound. Again he tapped the back wall of the bedstead, scowling at the set of small erotic pictures framed among the panelling. Then he pushed his cap back and pulled a hairpin from his top-knot. He pried with it among the grooves among the panels, without finding any deep fissure indicating a secret opening.

With a sigh the judge stepped down to the floor. It was completely incomprehensible. Smoothing down his long beard, he again studied the bedstead. An uneasy feeling took hold of him. Both the Academician and the Queen Flower had been marked by thin, long scratches. It was a very old building, was it possible that some queer animal housed there? He remembered strange stories he had read about large . . .

He quickly put the candle back on the table, and carefully shook out the bedcurtains. Then he knelt on the floor and peered under the bed. There was nothing, not even dust or cobwebs. Finally he lifted up a corner of the thick red rug. The tiled floor underneath was entirely free from dust. Evidently the room had been thoroughly swept after the Academician's death.

' Perhaps some queer beast came in from outside, through the barred window,' he muttered. He went to the sitting-room, took his long sword from the couch where Ma Joong had deposited it, and stepped out on the veranda. He prodded with the sword among the overhanging clusters of wistaria, then shook the mass of leaves vigorously. Clouds of blue blossoms came drifting down, but that was all.

Judge Dee went back to the Red Room. He pushed the door shut, and drew the centre table up against it. Then he loosened the sash round his waist and took off his upper robe. Having folded it up he put it on the floor, in front of the dressing-table. He quickly verified that the two candles would last through what was left of the night, then placed his cap on the table. He stretched himself out on the floor, his head on his folded robe, his right hand on the hilt of the drawn sword by his side. He was a light sleeper, he knew that the slightest noise would wake him.

# VI

After Ma Joong had said goodnight to the judge, he went to the hall of the hostel, where half a dozen waiters stood huddled together, discussing the tragedy in hushed voices. He grabbed an intelligent looking youngster by his arm and told him to show him the kitchen entrance.

The boy took him outside in the street and to a bamboo door in the fence to the left of the gatehouse. When they had gone inside there was on the right the blind outer wall of the hostel compound, on the left a neglected garden. From the door farther along in the wall came the sound of clattering platters and running water.

'That's the entrance of our kitchen,' the waiter said. 'We had a very late dinner, over in the right wing.'

'Walk on!' Ma Joong ordered.

Near the corner of the compound they found their progress barred by a dense, low shrubbery, overhung with clusters of wistaria. Ma Joong parted the branches, and saw a flight of narrow wooden steps, leading up to the left end of the veranda of the Red Pavilion. Below the steps was a path, overgrown with weeds.

'That leads to the back entrance of the Queen Flower's pavilion,' the waiter remarked, looking over Ma Joong's shoulder. 'That's where she receives her favourite admirers. It's a cosy place, beautifully furnished.'

Ma Joong grunted. With some difficulty he struggled through the dense shrubbery till he reached a thinner patch in front of the veranda. He could hear Judge Dee moving about in the Red Room. Turning round to the waiter, who was following close behind him, he laid his finger on his lips, then quickly searched the bushes. As an experienced woodsman he hardly made any sound. When he had verified that no one was hiding there, he moved on till he came out on a broad road.

'This is the main road of the park,' the youngster explained. 'If we keep to the right, we come out on the street again, on the other side of our hostel.'

Ma Joong nodded. He reflected with dismay that anyone could approach and enter the Red Pavilion from outside unnoticed. One moment he thought of passing the night right there, sleeping under a tree. But Judge Dee would have his own plans for action during the night, and the judge had ordered him to find himself a lodging somewhere else. Well, anyway, he had now made sure at least that no miscreants were lying in wait to disturb his master.

Back at the entrance of the hostel Ma Joong made the waiter explain to him how he could find the Blue Tower. It was located in the south section, somewhere behind the Crane Bower restaurant. Ma Joong pushed his cap back from his forehead and walked down the street.

Although it was past midnight all the gambling halls and restaurants were still brilliantly lighted, and the noisy crowd in the streets had hardly thinned. Having passed the Crane Bower, he turned to the left.

Here he found himself suddenly in a very quiet back street. The two-storied houses lining it were dark, and there was no one about. Studying the doorsigns, which indicated only a rank and a number, he understood that these were the dormitories of the courtesans and prostitutes, divided according to their respective ranks. These houses were barred to outsiders, here the girls ate and slept, and received their training in singing and dancing.

'The Blue Tower must be near by,' he muttered. 'Conveniently close to the source of supply!'

Suddenly he halted in his steps. From behind a shuttered window on his left came the sound of moaning. He pressed his ear to the wood. For a while all was quiet, then it started again. There must be somebody in distress, and probably all alone, too, for the inmates were not likely to return there before day-break. He quickly inspected the front door, marked 'Second Rank, no. 4'. It was locked, and made of solid boards. Ma Joong looked up at the narrow balcony that ran all along the front of the house. He tucked the slips of his robe under his belt, jumped up and got hold of the balcony's edge. He pulled himself up easily and climbed over the balustrade. Kicking in the first lattice-door he saw, he went into a small room that smelled of powder and rouge. He found a candle and a tinderbox on the dressing-table. He stepped out on the landing with the lighted candle and quickly went down the narrow staircase, into the dark hall.

A ray of light came from under the door on his left. The moans were coming from there. He put the candle down on the floor and went inside. It was a large, bare room lit only by one oil lamp. Six thick pillars supported the low, raftered ceiling, the floor was covered by reed mats. On the wall opposite him hung a row of guitars, bamboo flutes, violins and other musical instruments. It was evidently the training hall of the courtesans. The moans came from the farthest pillar, near the window. He quickly went there.

A naked girl was half hanging, half standing with her face to the pillar, her arms raised above her head. They were lashed to the pillar with a woman's silk sash. Her shapely back and hips showed red weals. A pair of wide trousers and a long trouser-cord were lying at her feet. As she heard him the girl cried out, without turning her head:

'No! Please don't . . .'

'Shut up!' Ma Joong told her gruffly. 'I have come to help you.'

Taking the knife from his girdle, he quickly cut the sash. The girl made a vain attempt to take hold of the pillar, then she collapsed on the floor. Cursing his clumsiness, Ma Joong

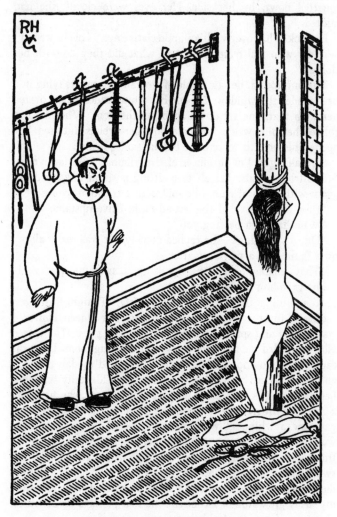

MA JOONG MAKES A DISCOVERY

squatted down by her side. Her eyes were closed, she had fainted.

He looked her over with an appreciative eye. 'Lovely wench! Wonder who maltreated her. And what did they do with her clothes?'

Turning round, he saw a pile of woman's garments lying in a heap under the window. He got her white under robe, covered her with that, and sat down again on the floor. When he had rubbed her blue wrists for some time her eyelids fluttered. She opened her mouth to scream, but he said quickly:

'It's all right. I'm an officer of the tribunal. Who are you?'

She tried to raise herself to a sitting position but lay down again with a cry of pain. She said with a trembling voice:

'I am a courtesan of the second rank. I live upstairs.'

'Who has been beating you?'

'Oh, it's nothing!' she replied quickly. 'It was really all my own fault. Just a private matter.'

'That remains to be seen. Speak up, answer my question!'

She gave him a frightened look.

'It's nothing, really,' she repeated softly. 'Tonight I attended a dinner, together with Autumn Moon, our Queen Flower. I was clumsy and spilled wine on the robe of a guest. The Queen Flower scolded me and sent me to our dressing-room. Later she came there too and took me here. She started to slap my face, and when I tried to ward off her blows I accidentally scratched her arms. She is very short-tempered, you know, she flew into a rage and ordered me to strip. She bound me to this pillar and gave me a whipping with my trouser-cord. She told me she would come back later and free me, when I had had time to think over my shortcomings.' Her lips began to tremble. She swallowed a few times before she went on: 'But . . . but she didn't come. At last I couldn't stand on my legs any more and my arms grew numb. I thought she had perhaps forgotten all about me. I was so afraid that . . .'

Tears came running down her cheeks. In her excitement she

had started to speak with a heavy accent. Ma Joong wiped her tears off with the tip of his sleeve and said in his own broad dialect:

'Your worries are over, Silver Fairy! A man from your own village shall now look after you!' Ignoring her astonished look, he went on: 'It was a lucky chance that made me pass by this house and hear your moans, for Autumn Moon won't come back. Not now or ever!'

She raised herself on her hands to a sitting position, not minding the dress that had dropped down from her naked torso. She asked in a tense voice:

'What happened to her?'

'She is dead,' Ma Joong replied soberly.

The girl buried her face in her hands, she started to cry again. Ma Joong shook his head perplexedly. He reflected sadly that you never knew with a woman.

Silver Fairy raised her head and said in a forlorn voice:

'Our Queen Flower dead! She was so beautiful and so clever. . . . Sometimes she would beat us, but she was often also so kind and understanding. She wasn't very strong. Did she suddenly become ill?'

'Heaven knows! Let's talk a bit about me now, shall we? I am the eldest son of the boatman Ma Liang, from the north of our village.'

'You don't say! So you are a son of Boatman Ma! I am the second daughter of Wu, of the butcher shop. I remember that he mentioned your father, said he was the best boatman on the river. How did you come here on the island?'

'I arrived here tonight, together with my boss, Judge Dee. He is the magistrate of the neighbour district Poo-yang, and now temporarily in charge here.'

'I know him. He was at the dinner I told you about. He seemed a nice, quiet man.'

'Nice he is,' Ma Joong agreed. 'But as to quiet—let me tell you he can be mighty lively, at times! Well, I'll carry you up to your room, we must do something about your back.'

'No, I won't stay in this house tonight!' the girl called out with a frightened look. 'Take me somewhere else!'

'If you tell me where! I only arrived tonight, and I was kept fairly busy, didn't yet get round to finding myself a place to stay.'

She bit her lips.

'Why is everything always so complicated?' she asked unhappily.

'Ask my boss, dear! I only do the rough jobs.'

She smiled faintly.

'All right, take me to the silk shop two streets up. It's kept by a widow called Wang, from our village. She'll let me stay there the night, and you too. Help me to the washroom first, though.'

Ma Joong made her stand up and put the white robe round her shoulders. He picked up her other clothes, and supporting her by her arm, took her to the bathroom at the back of the house.

'If anyone comes and asks after me, say that I have left!' she told him quickly before closing the door.

He waited in the corridor till she came out, fully dressed. Seeing how much difficulty she had in walking he picked her up in his arms. Following her instructions he carried her out into the alley behind the house, then through a narrow passage to the back door of a small shop. He put the girl down and knocked.

Silver Fairy hurriedly explained to the sturdy woman who opened that she wanted to stay there with her friend. The woman asked no questions but took them straight up to an attic, small but clean. Ma Joong told her to bring them a pot of hot tea, a towel and a box of ointment. He helped the girl to undress again, and to lie down on her belly on the narrow couch. When the widow returned and saw the girl's back, she cried out:

'You poor dear! What has happened to you?'

'I'll take care of that, auntie!' Ma Joong said and pushed her outside.

He put ointment on the weals on the girl's back with a practised hand. They didn't amount to much; he thought that all traces would have disappeared in a few days. But when he came to the bleeding sores on her hips he frowned angrily. He washed them with the tea and put ointment on them. Then he sat down on the only chair and said curtly:

'Those sores across your hips were never caused by a cord, my girl! I am an officer of the tribunal, and I know my job! Hadn't you better tell me the whole story?'

She pressed her face on her folded arms. Her back shook, she was sobbing. Ma Joong covered her up with the robe, then resumed:

'What games you girls play amongst yourselves is your own affair. Within reason, at least. But if an outsider maltreats you, that's very much the business of the tribunal. Come on, tell me who did it!'

Silver Fairy turned her tear-stained face to him.

'It's such a sordid story!' she muttered unhappily. 'Well, you'll know that girls of the third and fourth rank have to take any customer that pays the price, but that courtesans of the second and first ranks are allowed to choose their lovers. I belong to the second rank, I can't be forced to grant my favours to someone I don't like. But there are, of course, special cases, like that horrid old Wen, the curio-dealer. He is a very important man here, you know. He has tried to get me several times but I always managed to escape. At the dinner tonight he must have wormed out of Autumn Moon that she had left me tied to the pillar in the training hall, and the odious man came there not long after the Queen Flower had left. He said he would untie me if I did all kinds of sordid things, and when I refused he took one of the long bamboo flutes from the wall and started to beat me with it. Autumn Moon's whipping hadn't been too bad, it was the humiliation that counted more

59

than the pain. But that dirty Wen really wanted to hurt me, he left only when he had me screaming for mercy at the top of my voice and when I had promised I would do anything he liked. He said he would come back later for me, that's why I didn't want to stay in that house. Please don't tell anybody, Wen can completely ruin me, you know!'

'The mean bastard!' Ma Joong growled. 'Don't you worry, I'll get him, and without mentioning you. The wretched crook is mixed up in some shady business here, and he started as long ago as thirty years back! Nice long record!'

The widow had brought no cups, so he let the girl drink from the spout of the teapot. She thanked him, then said pensively:

'Wish I could help you, he has maltreated other girls here too.'

'Well, you wouldn't know about what happened here thirty years ago, dear!'

'That's true, I am just nineteen. But I know somebody who could tell you a lot about the old days. She is a poor old woman, a Miss Ling. I take singing lessons from her. She is blind, and she has a bad lung disease, but she has a very good memory. She lives in a hovel, over on the west side of the island, opposite the landing stage, and . . .'

'Would that be near the pumpkin patch of the Crab?'

'Yes! How could you possibly know that?'

'We officers of the tribunal know more than you'd think!' Ma Joong answered smugly.

'The Crab and the Shrimp are good fellows, they once helped me to get away from that horrid old curio-dealer. And the Shrimp is a formidable fighter.'

'The Crab, you mean.'

'No, the Shrimp. They say that six strong men wouldn't dare to attack the Shrimp.'

Ma Joong shrugged his shoulders. No use to argue with a woman about fighting. She went on:

'As a matter of fact, it was the Crab who introduced me to

Miss Ling, now and then he brings her medicine, for her cough. The poor dear's face is horribly disfigured by pock-marks, but she has the most beautiful voice. It seems that thirty years ago she was a famous courtesan here, of the first rank, and very popular. Isn't it sad that such an ugly old woman once was a great courtesan? It makes you think that some day you yourself . . .'

Her voice trailed off. In order to cheer her up Ma Joong began to talk about their village. It turned out that he had met her father once, in his shop on the marketplace. She said that later he had got into debt, and thus had had to sell his two daughters to a procurer.

The widow Wang came back with new tea and a platter of dried melon seeds and candy. They had an animated conversation about people they knew. When the widow had set out on a long story about her husband, Ma Joong suddenly noticed that Silver Fairy had fallen asleep.

'We'd better call it a day, auntie!' he said to the widow. 'I'll have to leave here tomorrow morning before dawn. Don't bother about breakfast, I'll pick up a few oil cakes in a street stall. Tell the girl that I'll try to pass by here again about noon.'

After the widow had gone down Ma Joong loosened his belt, stepped out of his boots and stretched himself out on the floor in front of the bed, his head on his folded arms. He was accustomed to sleeping in unusual places; soon he was snoring loudly.

# VII

In the Red Pavilion Judge Dee didn't find it so easy to get sleep on the floor. The red rug was but a poor substitute for the thick, springy bedmat of soft reed he was accustomed to. It took a long time before he dozed off.

But he didn't sleep well. He was visited by strange dreams, reflecting the uneasy thoughts about the Red Room that had flashed through his mind just before he laid himself down. He had lost his way in a dense, dark forest and was trying frantically to find a path through the thorny undergrowth. Suddenly something cold and scaly fell onto his neck. He grabbed the writhing thing, then threw it away with a curse. It was a large centipede. The animal must have bitten him, for he suddenly felt dizzy, everything grew black. When he came to he found himself lying on the bedstead of the Red Room, gasping for air. A formless dark shape was looming over him, pressing him down relentlessly and enveloping him in a foul, putrid smell. A black tentacle began to grope for his throat in the slow but purposeful manner of a blind beast that knows its prey can't escape. When he was nearly suffocating, the judge woke up with a start, drenched in perspiration.

He sighed with relief when he realized that it had only been a nightmare. He was going to sit up to wipe off his streaming face, when he suddenly checked himself. There was indeed a nauseating smell in the room, and the candles were no longer burning. At the same time he saw out of the corner of his eye a dark shape flitting past the barred window, faintly lit by the light from the park.

For one brief moment he thought he was dreaming again, then knew that he was fully awake. He tightened his grip on the hilt of his sword. Lying perfectly still, he peered intently at the window and the black shadows round it. He strained his ears. Then a furtive scratching came from the bedstead, followed by a flapping sound, near the ceiling above his head. At the same time a floorboard creaked, outside on the veranda.

Noiselessly the judge got up from the floor and remained there in a crouching position, his sword ready. When all remained silent, he suddenly leaped up and stood himself with his back to the wall, opposite the bedstead. A quick look around convinced him that the room was empty. The table was still standing against the door, where he had put it. In three strides he was over at the barred window. The veranda was deserted. The wistaria clusters were swinging to and fro in the breeze that had got up.

Sniffing the air, he noticed that the offensive smell was still there. But now he thought it might well have been caused by the smoke of the two candles, snuffed out by the draught.

He opened his tinderbox, relighted the candles, and took one over to the bedstead. He could see nothing unusual there. After he had kicked against one of the legs, he thought he could hear a faint sound of scratching again. It might be mice. Raising the candle he scrutinized the thick roofbeams. The flapping sound might have been caused by a bat that had been hanging there, and now had flown outside through the barred window. Only the dark shape he had seen there had been much larger than any bat could be. Sadly shaking his head, he pushed the table away from the door, and crossed the antechamber into the sitting-room.

The door leading to the veranda was wide open, as he had purposely left it to let the cool night air in. He stepped out on the veranda, and tested the floorboards with his foot. One of the boards in front of the barred window creaked, making exactly the same sound as he had heard.

He went to stand at the balustrade, looking out over the deserted park. The cool breeze moved the garlands of coloured lampions. It must be long past midnight now; no sound came from the park restaurant, but some of its second-floor windows were still lit. He reflected that the extinguished candles, the smell, the dark shape, and the scratching and flapping could all have a perfectly innocent explanation. But the creaking floorboard proved that something or someone had passed by the barred window.

The judge pulled his thin under-robe closer to him and went inside. He stretched himself out on the couch in the sitting-room. Now his fatigue asserted itself, soon he sank into a dreamless sleep.

He woke up when the bleak light of dawn was filling the room. A waiter was hovering about near the table, preparing hot tea. Judge Dee told him to serve his morning rice out on the veranda. The coolness of the night still lingered on, but as the sun gained strength it would soon become hot again.

The judge selected a clean under-robe, then went to the hostel's bathroom. At this early hour he had the sunken pool all to himself, and he let himself soak there for a long time. When he came back in the Red Pavilion he found a bowl of rice and a platter of salted vegetables standing ready on the small table on the veranda. He was just taking up his chopsticks when the wistaria clusters at the veranda's right end were swept aside. Ma Joong appeared and wished the judge a good morning.

'Where did you come from?' Judge Dee asked, astonished.

'Last night I had a quick look around, sir. I found that there's a sidepath of the main park road that leads to this veranda. From the left end another path goes straight to the Queen Flower's pavilion. So she spoke the truth, for once, when last night she said that this veranda here affords a short-cut to her place. It also explains how she could come here and to the Red Room without the people of the hostel knowing about it. Did Your Honour sleep well?'

Munching a piece of salted cabbage, the judge decided that he'd better not tell Ma Joong his doubts about what he had

64

seen and heard during the night. He knew that ghostly phenomena were the only thing his stalwart lieutenant was really afraid of. So he answered:

'Fairly well, thank you. Did you have any luck on the landing stage?'

'I did and I didn't! I arrived there at dawn; the fishermen were getting ready to set out. Feng's junk was standing on shore, the boatmen were starting to paint her repaired hulk. The captain is a cheerful soul, he showed me over the ship. She carries plenty of sail, and the cabins in the stern are as comfortable as those in a hostel; they have a broad balcony too. When I asked about the collision, the captain grew red in his face and used some pretty strong language. They were rammed by the other boat towards midnight, it was entirely the fault of the Academician's boatmen, their skipper was drunk as a lord. But the Academician himself was fairly sober. Miss Feng had rushed out on the balcony in her nightrobe, thinking that her boat was foundering. The Academician went up to her and personally apologized, the captain saw them standing together in front of her cabin.

'Well, the boatmen were busy all night, getting the two ships clear. It was only towards daybreak that they got things in such a shape that the Academician's junk could tow the other ship to the landing stage. There was only one sedan chair there, and Miss Feng and her maid rented that one. It took some time till palankeens arrived to bring Lee and his boon companions to this hostel. While waiting for them the five gentlemen sat in the main cabin, nursing their hangovers. But the Academician was fairly chipper, he walked about on the landing stage. Nobody saw the curio-dealer, though.'

'Probably your friends the Crab and the Shrimp just made up that story, to say something nasty about Wen,' Judge Dee said indifferently.

'Maybe. But they didn't lie about their pumpkin patch. There was a bit of mist over the river, but I could see the Crab and the Shrimp pottering about there. Don't know what the Shrimp was at, the small fellow was hopping around like mad. By the way, I also saw that leper, sir. He was standing there, shouting at a boatman because he refused to take him up river. Must say the poor beggar cursed like a real gentleman, it was a treat to listen to him! Finally he showed the boatman a silver piece, but the man said he preferred to remain poor but healthy. The leper went off in a huff.'

'At least the unfortunate wretch isn't pressed for money,' the judge remarked. 'Last night he didn't take the coppers I offered him.'

Ma Joong rubbed his heavy chin, then resumed:

'Coming back to last night, Your Honour, I happened to run into a courtesan called Silver Fairy, she said she had met you in the Crane Bower.' As Judge Dee nodded, Ma Joong told him about his discovering her in the training hall, and how first Autumn Moon and then Wen Yuan had maltreated her.

'Autumn Moon warned that foul curio-dealer that the girl was at his mercy!' Judge Dee said angrily. 'I saw her whisper to him when she came back to the dinner party. The woman had a nasty cruel streak in her.' He tugged at his moustache, then added: 'Anyway, the problem of those scratches on the Queen Flower's arms has now been solved. Did you see to it that the girl was put up for the night in a safe place?'

'Oh yes, sir. I took her to a widow, an old friend of hers.' Fearing that the judge would inquire where he had passed the night himself, he went on quickly: 'Silver Fairy takes singing lessons from a Miss Ling, a former courtesan to whom the Crab introduced her. Miss Ling is now an old and sick woman, but thirty years ago she was a famous beauty here. If Your Honour should want to look further into the suicide of Tao Pan-te's father, Miss Ling might be able to supply more details.'

'You did very well, Ma Joong. As regards that old suicide, it happened a long time ago, but right here in this Red Pavilion.

Every bit of information on this queer place is welcome. Do you know where to find Miss Ling?'

'She lives somewhere near the Crab's place, I could ask him.'

Judge Dee nodded. He told Ma Joong to lay out his green ceremonial robe, and order the manager to have a rented palankeen standing ready to take them to Feng's mansion.

Ma Joong went to the hall, humming a tune. Silver Fairy had not yet woken up when he left, but even in her sleep she had looked remarkably attractive, he thought. He hoped to see her again at noon. 'Funny I got so fond of that wench,' he muttered. 'Only thing I did with her is talking! Must be because she's from my native village!'

# VIII

Judge Dee and Ma Joong stepped down from the palankeen in front of the magnificent temple on the north side of the main street. The judge had already noticed the high red pillars in front of the sumptuous marble portal when he passed by there the day before, on his arrival at Paradise Island.

'What deity is this temple dedicated to?' he asked the chief bearer.

'To the God of Wealth, Excellency! Every visitor to the island prays and burns incense there before he goes to try his luck at the gaming tables.'

Feng Dai's residence was directly opposite. It was an extensive compound, surrounded by a high wall, newly plastered. Feng came to meet the judge in the front courtyard, paved with slabs of white marble. Across it stood a large two-storied building, with a monumental gatehouse of carved wood and roofs decked with copper tiles that glistened in the morning sun.

While Feng conducted the judge to his library to refresh himself, his house steward took Ma Joong to the warden's office in the east wing, so that he could verify that everything was in readiness for the court session there.

Feng ushered Judge Dee into a large, richly furnished room, and bade him sit down at the antique tea table of carved blackwood. While sipping the fragrant tea the judge looked with interest at the bookshelves that took up the wall opposite him. They were loaded with books, some of them bristling with paper markers. Feng, who had followed his glance, said with a deprecating smile:

'I myself can't say that I am much of a scholar, Your Honour! I bought those books in the old days, chiefly because I thought that a library ought to have books in it! I use this as

68

a reception room, really. But my friend Tao Pan-te often comes to consult the books, he is interested in history and philosophy. And my daughter Jade Ring uses them too. She has acquired some skill in composing poetry, and she is very fond of reading.'

'Then her marrying the poet Kia Yu-po will truly be "a literary union predestined by Heaven", as they say,' Judge Dee remarked with a smile. 'I hear that the youngster was rather unlucky at the tables, but he comes from a rich family, I suppose.'

'No, he doesn't. He lost practically everything he had, as a matter of fact. In this particular case, however, fortune resulted from misfortune! When Kia paid me a visit to negotiate a loan that would enable him to continue his journey to the capital, my daughter happened to see him and then and there fell in love with him. That pleased me, for she'll soon be nineteen, and till now she has always refused the candidates proposed to her. I invited Kia a few times here to my house, and contrived that he also saw my daughter. Then Tao Pan-te told me that Kia had seemed much impressed by Jade Ring, and Tao acted as middle-man for arranging their betrothal. As to the financial aspects, I am considered a wealthy man, sir, and the happiness of my only daughter is all I care for. As my son-in-law, Kia'll have plenty and to spare!' He paused. He cleared his throat and asked, after some hesitation: 'Did Your Honour already form an opinion on the shocking death of the Queen Flower?'

'I never try to form an opinion before I know all the facts,' the judge replied curtly. 'Presently we shall hear the result of the autopsy. I also want to know more about the man who killed himself because of her, the Academician Lee Lien. Tell me what kind of man he was!'

Feng tugged pensively at his long sidewhiskers.

'I met him only once,' he replied slowly, 'that was on the 19th, when he came to see me about settling the damage caused by a collision on the river, involving my boat and his. He was a handsome but haughty man, very conscious of his own importance, I thought. I let him off lightly, for I used to know his father, Dr Lee Wei-djing. That was a fine, upstanding man in his younger years! Good-looking, strong as an ox, witty in his conversation, and a polished man of the world. In the olden days, when he stayed here on the island on his way to and from the capital, all the courtesans ran after him. But he knew better! Being a candidate for a Censorship, he realized that his morals must be irreproachable. Left quite a few broken hearts here, I dare say! Well, as Your Honour probably knows, twenty-five years ago he married the daughter of a high official, and was appointed Imperial Censor. Six years ago he retired, and settled down on the family estate, in the mountainous region up north here. Unfortunately the family suffered some financial reverses, on account of bad harvests and unlucky investments, I heard. But their landed property still provides an ample income, I suppose.'

'I have never met Dr Lee,' the judge said, 'but I know that he was a capable official. It's a pity that bad health forced him to retire. What ailment is he suffering from?'

'That I don't know, sir. It must be serious, though, for I heard that he has been confined to his house for nearly a year already. That's why, as I told Your Honour last night, it was an uncle who came here to fetch the Academician's dead body.'

'Some people say,' Judge Dee resumed, 'that the Academician was not the type of man to commit suicide because of a woman.'

'Not because of a woman,' Feng said with a sly smile, 'but because of himself! As I told Your Honour, he was an extremely conceited person. The Queen Flower's refusing him would be talked about all over the province, therefore it was wounded pride that made him kill himself, I think.'

'You may be right there,' the judge agreed. 'By the way, did the uncle take away with him all the Academician's papers?'

Feng clapped his hand to his forehead.

'That reminds me!' he exclaimed. 'I forgot to give him the documents found on the deceased's table.' He rose and took from the drawer in his desk a package wrapped up in brown paper. Judge Dee opened it and glanced through the contents. After a while he looked up and remarked:

'The Academician was a methodical man. He carefully recorded all expenses incurred during his stay here, including even the fees of the women he slept with. I see here the names of Jade Flower, Carnation and Peony.'

'All courtesans of the second rank,' Feng explained.

'He settled his bill with those three women on the 25th, I see. But there's no record here of any payment made to Autumn Moon.'

'She attended most of the Academician's parties,' Feng said, 'but the fees for that are always included in the bill of the restaurant. As to their ah . . . more intimate relations, in the case of a courtesan of the first rank, as Autumn Moon was, the customer gives her a present, at parting. It glosses over the um . . . ah . . . commercial aspects of the attachment.' Feng looked pained, he evidently thought it beneath his dignity to discuss the cruder aspects of his business. He quickly selected one sheet from those in front of the judge, and went on: 'These are the Academician's scribblings, proving that his last thoughts were devoted to our Queen Flower. It was for that reason that I summoned her, whereupon she revealed that he had offered to redeem her, and that she had refused.'

Judge Dee studied the sheet. Apparently the Academician had first tried to draw a complete circle in one brush stroke. He had repeated the effort, then written underneath three times the two words 'Autumn Moon'. Putting the paper in his sleeve, he got up, and said:

'We shall now proceed to the court room.'

The warden's offices took up the entire east wing of the compound. Feng led the judge through the chancery, where four clerks were busily wielding their writing brushes, to a large, high-ceilinged hall. The open front, lined with red-lacquered pillars, faced a well-tended flower garden. Half a dozen men stood waiting there. The judge recognized Tao Pan-te, the curio-dealer Wen Yuan, and the poet Kia Yu-po. The other three he didn't know.

When he had answered their bows, Judge Dee sat down in the high armchair behind the bench. With a sour look he took in the luxurious appointments of this court hall. The bench was covered with costly red brocade, embroidered in gold, and the writing implements lying ready on it were all valuable antiques. The beautifully carved stone inkslab, the paper weight of green jade, the sandalwood seal box, and the writing brushes with the ivory shafts belonged to a collector's studio rather than to a tribunal. The floor consisted of coloured tiles, and the back wall was hidden by a magnificent high folding screen, painted in gold and blue with a design of waves and clouds. Judge Dee held the view that public offices ought to be as simple as possible, in order to show the people that the government doesn't waste its tax-money on unnecessary luxury. But on Paradise Island evidently even government offices had to show off the place's enormous wealth.

Feng Dai and Ma Joong remained standing, each at one end of the bench. The recording clerk had sat down at a lower table against the side wall, and two of the men unknown to the judge now took up their positions on the right and left before the bench. The long bamboo staffs they carried proclaimed them to be two of the warden's special constables.

The judge looked through the papers that had been put ready for him, then rapped the gavel and spoke:

'I, Assessor of the tribunal of Chin-hwa, declare the session open. I shall begin with the case of the Academician Lee Lien. I have here before me the draft of a death certificate drawn up by His Excellency Magistrate Lo, stating that the said Academi-cian killed himself on the 25th, having become despondent over his unrequited love for the courtesan Autumn Moon, this year's Queen Flower of Paradise Island. I see from the autopsy report appended thereto that the Academician killed himself by cutting his right jugular vein with his own dagger. On the face and forearms of the deceased were found thin scratches. The deceased had no bodily defects, but two swollen places were discovered on either side of his neck, of undetermined origin.' The judge looked up and said: 'Let the coroner come forward. I want a detailed report on those swellings.'

An elderly man with a pointed beard came to the bench. He knelt down and began:

'This person respectfully reports that he is the owner of the pharmacy of this island, and concurrently coroner of this court. As regards the swollen places found on the Academician's body, I beg to state that they were located on either side of the neck, under the ears. They had the size of a large marble. The skin was not discoloured, and since there were no holes or punctures, the swelling must be ascribed to some internal cause.'

'I see,' Judge Dee said. 'After I have verified a few details, I shall have this suicide duly registered.' He rapped his gavel. 'Second, this court has to consider the demise of the courtesan Autumn Moon, which occurred last night in the Red Pavilion. I shall now hear the report on the autopsy.'

'This person,' the coroner spoke up again, 'examined at midnight the dead body of Miss Yuan Feng, called Autumn Moon. He found that death was due to heart failure, presumably caused by over-indulgence in alcohol.'

The judge raised his eyebrows. He said curtly:

'I want further comment on that statement.'

'During the last two months, Your Honour, the deceased consulted me twice regarding dizziness and palpitations of the heart. I found that she was in a run-down condition, prescribed a soothing medicine, and advised her to take a rest and abstain from intoxicants. I reported this also to the office of the brothel guild. I am informed, however, that the deceased confined herself to taking my medicine, and did not change her mode of living.'

'I urged her to obey the doctor's orders to the letter, Your Honour,' Feng remarked hurriedly. 'We always insist that the professional women here follow medical advice, both in their own interest and ours. But she wouldn't listen, and, since she is the Queen Flower . . .'

Judge Dee nodded. 'Proceed!' he ordered the coroner.

'Apart from the blue spots on her throat, and a few scratches on her arms, the body of the deceased showed no signs of violence. Since this person was informed that last night she drank excessively, he arrived at the conclusion that, after she had laid herself down to sleep, she suddenly got short of breath. She jumped down from the bedstead and, in a frantic attempt to get air, caught with both hands at her own throat. Then she collapsed on the floor, in her last agony clawing at the carpet, as proved by the bits of red fluff I found under her fingernails. On the basis of these facts, Your Honour, I arrived at the conclusion that death was caused by a sudden heart attack.'

On a sign of the judge the clerk read out the coroner's statement as he had noted it down. When the coroner had affixed his thumbmark to it, Judge Dee dismissed him and asked Feng:

'What do you know about the courtesan's antecedents?'

Feng Dai took a sheaf of papers from his sleeve and replied:

'Early this morning I had all her papers sent over here from our main office, sir.' He consulted the documents and went on: 'She was the daughter of a small official in the capital, who sold her to a wine house when he got into debt. Being a well-educated and clever girl, she thought that being a prostitute attached to a wine house didn't offer her sufficient scope for her talents, and she began to sulk. Her owner then sold her to a procurer, for two gold bars. He brought her here to the island, and when our purchasing committee had seen her dance and heard her sing she was bought for three gold bars. That was about two years ago. She at once began to cultivate prominent

JUDGE DEE, ASSISTED BY WARDEN FENG, HEARS KIA YU-PO

scholars and artists who passed through here, and quickly became one of the leading courtesans. Four months ago, when the committee for choosing this year's Queen Flower met, she was unanimously elected. I see that there were never any complaints lodged against her, and she never got involved in any trouble.'

'All right,' Judge Dee said. 'You shall inform the next of kin of the dead woman that they can come to fetch the corpse, for burial. I now want to hear the testimony of the curio-dealer Wen Yuan.'

Wen gave the judge a bewildered look. When he had knelt down in front of the bench, Judge Dee ordered:

'Describe your movements after you had left the dinner in the Crane Bower!'

'This person left the dinner early, Your Honour, because he had an appointment with an important client. It was to discuss the purchase of a valuable antique painting, as a matter of fact. From the restaurant I went directly to my curio-shop.'

'Who was that client, and how long did he stay with you?'

'It was the Commissioner Hwang, Your Honour, who is now staying in the second hostel in this same street. But I waited for him in vain. When I went to see him just now, on my way here, he maintained that our appointment had not been for yesterday, but for tonight. I must have misunderstood him when talking with him two days ago.'

'Quite,' Judge Dee said. He gave a sign to the clerk, who read out Wen's statement. The curio-dealer agreed that it was correct and impressed his thumbmark on it. The judge dismissed him, and called Kia Yu-po before the bench. He spoke:

'The Candidate Kia Yu-po shall now state what he did after he had left the dinner.'

'This person,' Kia began, 'has the honour to report that he left the dinner earlier because he wasn't feeling well. He intended to proceed to the restaurant's bathroom, but by mistake went to the dressing-room of the courtesans. He asked a waiter to direct him to the bathroom, then left the restaurant

76

and went on foot to the park. He walked around there till about the hour of midnight. Then he felt much better, and returned to his hostel.'

'It shall be so recorded,' Judge Dee said. When the poet had marked the clerk's notes with his thumbprint, the judge rapped his gavel and announced:

'The case of the demise of the courtesan Autumn Moon remains pending until further notice.'

Thereupon he closed the session. Before getting up he bent over to Ma Joong and whispered:

'Go and see that Commissioner Hwang. Then run over to the Crane Bower and to Kia's hostel and verify his statement. Come back here to report.' Turning to Feng Dai, he said: 'I want to have a private conversation with Mr Tao. Can you take us to a room where we shan't be disturbed?'

'Certainly sir! I'll take Your Honour to the garden pavilion. It's located in our backyard, close by my women's quarters; nobody from outside ever goes there.' He hesitated a moment, then continued, rather diffidently: 'If I may be permitted to say so, sir, I don't quite understand why Your Honour has decided to keep both cases pending. A plain case of suicide, and a death caused by heart failure . . . I would have thought that . . .'

'Oh,' Judge Dee said vaguely, 'only because I want to know something more about the background of those cases. Just to round them off, so to speak.'

## IX

The pavilion stood in the back of an extensive flower garden, it was half hidden by the tall oleander shrubs planted around it. Judge Dee sat down in the armchair in front of a high screen, decorated with a painting of plum blossoms. He motioned Tao Pan-te to take the chair by the small round table, where Feng's steward had placed the tea-tray and a platter of candied fruit.

It was very quiet in this secluded corner of the compound; there was only the humming of bees flying leisurely among the white oleander blossoms.

Tao Pan-te waited respectfully till the judge would open the conversation. After he had taken a few sips from his tea, Judge Dee began affably:

'I hear, Mr Tao, that you are known as a man of letters. Does your wine business and your household leave you sufficient leisure for literary pursuits?'

'I am fortunate in having a dependable and experienced staff, Your Honour. All the routine business connected with my wine shops and restaurants I can leave to them. And, since I am unmarried, the administration of my household is quite simple.'

'Allow me to come now straight to my subject, Mr Tao. I want to tell you, in the strictest confidence of course, that I suspect that both the Academician and the Queen Flower were murdered.'

He watched Tao closely when saying this, but the impassive face of the wine merchant didn't change. He asked calmly:

'How then does Your Honour explain the fact that in neither of the two cases could anybody have entered the room?'

'I can't! But neither can I explain how the Academician, who on five nights in succession had slept with other women, suddenly became so deeply infatuated with the Queen Flower

78

that he took his own life when she wouldn't have him! And neither can I understand why the Queen Flower, when catching at her own throat, didn't leave the marks of her long, pointed nails on her skin. There's more to these two cases than meets the eye, Mr Tao.' As Tao nodded slowly, the judge resumed: 'As yet I only have some vague theories. I think, however, that your father's suicide, which I am told took place in the same Red Pavilion, and under practically the same circumstances as that of the Academician, might provide a clue. I fully realize how painful this subject must be for you, but . . .' He let his voice trail off.

Tao Pan-te made no reply; he was deep in thought. At last he seemed to have reached a decision. He looked up and said in his quiet voice:

'My father didn't commit suicide, Your Honour. He was murdered. That knowledge has cast a dark shadow over my entire life, a shadow which will vanish only after I have succeeded in finding the foul murderer and have brought him to justice. For a son shall not live under one sky with his father's murderer.'

He paused. Looking straight ahead of him, he continued: 'I was a boy of ten when it happened. Yet I remember every small detail, having gone over it again and again, thousands of times, in the ensuing years. My father was very fond of me, his only son, and taught me himself. On the afternoon of that fatal day he had been teaching me history. Towards dusk he received a message, and told me he had to go at once to the Red Pavilion, in the Hostel of Eternal Bliss. After he had left I took up the book he had been reading aloud from and found his folding fan. I knew my father was very fond of that fan, so I ran out to take it to him. I had never been in that hostel before, but the manager knew me and told me to walk straight on to the Red Pavilion.

'I found the door standing ajar, went in and saw the Red Room. My father was lying slumped back in the armchair, in

79

front of the bed, on the right. Out of the corner of my eye I saw another person, clad in a long red robe, standing in the left corner. But I didn't pay any attention to him, for I was staring in speechless horror at the blood that was covering my father's breast. I ran up to him, and saw that he was dead. A small dagger was stuck in the left side of his throat. Half-distracted with fright and grief, I turned round to ask the other person what had happened. But he wasn't there any more. I rushed out of the room to find someone, but I stumbled in the corridor, my head must have hit the wall or a pillar. For when I came to I was lying in my own bedroom, in our summer villa in the mountains. The maid told me that I had been ill, and that my mother had moved the entire household to the villa because a smallpox epidemic was ravaging the island. She added that my father had left, on a long journey. Thus I thought that it had all been only a bad nightmare. But its horrible details remained engraved on my memory.'

He groped for his tea cup and took a long draught, then went on:

'Later, when I had grown up, I was told that my father had committed suicide, having locked himself alone in the Red Room. But I understood at once that he had been murdered, and that I had seen the murderer, just when he had done the foul deed. After I had rushed out, the criminal fled, locking the door behind him. He must have thrown the key inside through the barred window, for I was told that it was found on the floor, on the inside of the door.'

Tao sighed. He passed his hand over his eyes and resumed wearily:

'I then began, very discreetly, an investigation. But every attempt led to a dead end. To begin with, all the official records of the case were lost. The then magistrate of Chin-hwa, a wise and energetic official, had recognized that the brothels were mainly responsible for the quick spread of the smallpox epidemic. He had made all the women vacate them, and had had the entire quarter burned down. The warden's office caught fire also, and the files stored there went up in flames. I did find out, however, that my father had been in love with a courtesan called Green Jade, who had just been chosen Queen Flower. She had been a remarkable beauty, I was told, but she caught the disease soon after my father's death and died a few days later. The official version of my father's death was that he had killed himself because Green Jade had rebuffed him. Some persons who had been present when the magistrate heard Green Jade, just before she fell ill, assured me that the courtesan had stated that on the day before my father died she had informed him that she couldn't accept his offer to redeem her because she loved another man. Unfortunately the magistrate didn't ask her who that was. He only asked why my father had gone to the Red Room to commit suicide, and she replied that it must have been because she had often met him there.

'I thought that the murderer's motive might give me a clue to his identity. I was told that two other men had sought Green Jade's favours. Feng Dai, who was then twenty-four, and the curio-dealer Wen Yuan, at that time about thirty-five. Wen had already been married for eight years without having any offspring; it was common knowledge that he was incapable of exercising his marital duties, and among the courtesans it was well known that he sought a vicarious satisfaction in humiliating and hurting women. He courted Green Jade only because he wanted to assert himself as an elegant man of the world. That left Feng Dai, who was a handsome bachelor then, and deeply in love with Green Jade. It was said that he planned to marry her as his First Wife.'

Tao fell silent. He stared with unseeing eyes at the flowering bushes. Judge Dee casually turned his head to look at the screen. He had heard a rustling sound behind it. He strained his ears, but all was still again. He thought it must have been some dry leaves fluttering down. Then Tao fixed the judge with his large, melancholy eyes and resumed:

'Vague rumours hinted at Feng having murdered my father. That it was Feng who had been Green Jade's preferred lover, that he had met my father in the Red Room, and there killed him during a violent quarrel. Wen Yuan kept making veiled suggestions that he knew that was true. But when I pressed him for proof, he could only say that Green Jade had known it too, but had confirmed the suicide version in order to protect Feng. He added that he himself had seen Feng in the park, behind the Red Pavilion, at the time my father died. Thus all facts seemed to point at Feng.

'Words fail me to describe, sir, how deeply this conclusion shocked me. Feng had been my father's best friend, and after my father's death he had become my mother's trusted counsellor. When she had died and I had come of age, Feng helped me to continue my father's business; he has always been as a second father to me. Was he my father's murderer, who treated his victim's family so kindly only because of remorse? Or were the rumours, kept alive by Feng's enemy Wen Yuan, only malicious slander? Thus I have been torn by doubt, all these years. I have to associate daily with Feng, sir. Of course I never let him know my terrible suspicions. But all the time I am watching him, waiting for a word, a gesture that will prove him to be my father's murderer. I really can't . . .'

His voice broke, he buried his face in his hands.

Judge Dee remained silent. He thought he had heard again that faint sound behind the screen. This time it resembled the rustling of silk. He listened intently. As all remained quiet, he said gravely:

'I am grateful that you told me all this, Mr Tao. There is indeed a strong resemblance to the Academician's alleged suicide. I shall study carefully all the implications. For the moment I confine myself to verifying a few details. In the first place, why did the magistrate who dealt with the case rule that it had been suicide? You said he was a wise and competent official. He must surely have realized, just as you did later, that, although the room was locked, the key could have been thrown inside through the window or slipped through the crack under the door?'

Tao looked up. He answered listlessly:

'Just at that time the magistrate had his hands full with the smallpox epidemic, sir. It is said that people were dying like rats, the corpses were lying piled up by the roadside. My father's relationship with Green Jade was well known, one can imagine that, having heard her statement, he thought it provided a simple and welcome solution.'

'When you related that terrible boyhood experience,' the judge resumed, 'you stated that, when you entered the Red Room, the bedstead was on your right. At present, however, it is standing against the wall on the left. Are you sure you saw it on the right?'

'Absolutely, sir! That scene is for ever before my mind's eye. Perhaps the management shifted the furniture about later.'

'I'll look into that. One last question. You got only a glimpse of the person in the red robe, but you saw at least whether it was a man or a woman, I suppose?'

Tao shook his head disconsolately.

'I couldn't, Your Honour. I only remember it was rather a tall person, and clad in a red robe. I have tried to verify whether someone wearing such a robe has been seen at the time in or near the Hostel of Eternal Bliss, but in vain.'

'Red is rarely worn by men,' Judge Dee remarked pensively, 'and decent girls wear a red dress only once, and that is on their wedding day. One would conclude, therefore, that the third person in that room was a courtesan.'

'That's what I thought too, sir! I did my utmost to find out whether Green Jade had sometimes worn a red dress. But nobody had ever seen her wearing red, she preferred green, because of her name.'

Tao fell silent. He pulled at his short moustache, then went on:

'I would have left this island long ago, were it not that I know I shan't be able to find rest anywhere as long as this riddle has not been solved. I also feel that, by continuing the business which my father built up here, I am fulfilling at least part of my filial duty. But I find life here very difficult, sir. Feng is always so kind to me, and his . . .' He suddenly broke off. Giving the judge a quick look, he continued: 'You'll now understand that I can't claim any merit for my literary hobbies; they are only an attempt at escape, sir. An escape from a reality that bewilders, and often frightens me . . .'

He averted his eyes, evidently he kept himself under control with difficulty. In order to change the subject, Judge Dee asked:

'Have you any idea who could have hated the present Queen Flower, Autumn Moon, deeply enough to want to murder her?'

Tao shook his head. He answered:

'I take no part in the hectic night life here, sir, and I have met the Queen Flower only at official functions. She impressed me as being a shallow and fickle woman, but nearly all of the courtesans are that way, or have become so because of their unfortunate profession. She was popular, and attended some party or other practically every night. I have heard that, until she was chosen Queen Flower a few months ago, she was rather liberal with her favours. Afterwards, however, she would sleep only with special patrons, distinguished and wealthy persons, and they had to court her assiduously before she consented. None of those affairs developed into a regular liaison, as far as I know, and I never heard that anybody offered to redeem her. I presume that her sharp tongue deterred her clients. The Academician seems to have been the first to offer to buy her out. If someone hated her, the reason must lie in the past. Before she came to the island, at any rate.'

'I see. Well, I won't detain you any longer, Mr Tao. I'll just stay here a while to finish my tea. Please tell Mr Feng that I'll come to his office presently.'

A MEETING IN A GARDEN PAVILION

As soon as Tao was out of earshot, the judge sprang up and looked behind the screen. The slightly built girl standing there uttered a suppressed cry. She glanced wildly about her, then turned to the flight of steps that led down into the shrubbery at the back of the pavilion. Judge Dee grabbed her arm and pulled her back. He asked sternly:

'Who are you, and why were you eavesdropping?'

She bit her lips and looked up angrily at the judge. She had a regular, intelligent face, with large expressive eyes and long, curved eyebrows. She wore her hair combed straight back, gathered in a chignon at her neck. Her black damask robe was of simple style, but it went very well with her slender, shapely figure. The only ornaments she wore were two ear-pendants of green jade, and she carried a long, red scarf round her shoulders. She shook Judge Dee's hand from her arm and burst out:

'That hateful, despicable man Tao! How dare he slander my father! I hate him!'

She stamped her small foot on the floor.

'Calm yourself, Miss Feng!' Judge Dee said curtly. 'Sit down and have a cup of tea.'

'I won't!' she snapped. 'I only want to tell you, once and for all, that my father had nothing to do with the death of that Tao Kwang. Absolutely nothing, do you hear? No matter what that loathsome old toad of a curio-dealer may say. And tell Tao that I never want to see him again, never! And that I love Kia Yu-po, and that I am going to marry him as soon as I can, and without Tao or any other middleman! That's all!'

'Quite a tall order!' the judge said mildly. 'I wager that you gave the Academician a good tongue-lashing!'

She had been turning to go, but now she stood stock still. Fixing the judge with blazing eyes, she asked sharply:

'What do you mean by that?'

'Well,' Judge Dee said soothingly, 'the collision on the river was the fault of the Academician's boatmen, and it delayed your coming home one whole night, didn't it? Seeing that you are not burdened by an excessive amount of shyness, I imagine that you gave him a good piece of your mind.'

She tossed her head back and said contemptuously:

'You are completely wrong! Mr Lee apologized like a gentleman, and I accepted his apologies.'

She rushed down the front steps and disappeared among the flowering oleander shrubs.

# X

Judge Dee sat down again and slowly emptied his tea cup. Gradually he was getting an interesting insight into the relations of all these people. But it didn't help much in solving any of his problems.

He rose with a sigh and strolled back to the warden's office.

Feng Dai was waiting there for him, together with Ma Joong. Feng conducted them ceremoniously to the palankeen.

When they were being carried away, Ma Joong said:

'That old curio-dealer lied, of course, when he said at the session that he went home straight from the banquet—that we knew already. But the rest of his statement fits more or less, I am sorry to say! Commissioner Hwang told me that he had indeed an appointment with Wen, for this evening, he thought. But now that Wen maintains that it was for last night, Hwang admits that he may have been wrong. So that is Wen. As to Kia Yu-po, his statement was a bit sketchy, so to speak. The old hag in charge of the courtesan's dressing-room didn't have at all the impression that Kia entered there by mistake. For the first thing he asked was whether Autumn Moon and Silver Fairy were there. When she replied that they had left together, he turned round and rushed out without another word. The manager of the inn Kia is staying in—that small hostel next door to ours—told me that he happened to see Kia pass by when he was standing in front of his door, about half an hour or so before midnight that was. He had expected Kia to turn in, but the fellow walked on and entered the alley to the left of the hostel. And that alley leads to the pavilion of the Queen Flower—now deceased. Kia came back home towards midnight, the manager said.'

'Curious story!' Judge Dee remarked. Then he told Ma Joong

what Tao Pan-te had said about his father's alleged murder, and his suspicions of Feng Dai. Ma Joong doubtfully shook his large head.

'It'll take some time to sort all that out!' he said.

The judge made no comment. He remained deep in thought the rest of the way.

When they had stepped down from the palankeen in front of the Hostel of Eternal Bliss and were entering the hall, the portly innkeeper came up to Ma Joong and said, rather doubtfully:

'Two eh . . . gentlemen would like to have a word with you, Mr Ma. They are waiting in the kitchen. It's about salted fish, they said.'

For a moment Ma Joong stared at him, dumbfounded. Then he suddenly grinned broadly. He asked the judge:

'May I go and hear what they have to say, sir?'

'By all means. There's a point I want to verify with our host here. Come to the Red Pavilion when you are through.'

While Judge Dee beckoned the innkeeper, a waiter took Ma Joong to the kitchen.

Two cooks, their muscular torsos bare, were sourly watching the Crab, who was standing in front of the largest stove, a flat frying pan in his hand. The Shrimp and four scullery boys were looking on from a safe distance. The giant threw a big flat-fish high up in the air, then neatly caught it on its other side, right in the centre of the pan.

Looking with his bulging eyes at the two cooks, he said gravely:

'Now you have seen how it ought to be done. It's a flip, from the wrist. Now you do it, Shrimp!'

The small hunchback, looking furious, stepped forward and took the pan over from the Crab. He threw the fish up. It fell back in the pan, half of it lying over the rim.

'Twisted again!' the Crab said reproachfully. 'You twist

because you use your elbow. It should be a flip from the wrist.'
Noticing Ma Joong, he motioned him with his head to the open
kitchen door. He continued to the Shrimp: 'Go on, try it
again!' and pulled Ma Joong outside.

When they were standing in a corner of the neglected side
garden, he whispered hoarsely:

'Me and the Shrimp had business hereabouts, matter of a
fellow who cheated at the tables. Would you like to see that
curio-dealer, Mr Ma?'

'Not on your life! Seen his ugly mug already this morning.
That'll last me for a couple of years!'

'Now, let's suppose, just for the sake of argument,' the
Crab went on stolidly, 'that your boss wanted to see him. Then
he'd have to be quick, for Wen is leaving town tonight, I heard.
For the capital. To buy antiques, he says. I won't guarantee it's
true. Take it as an informal, voluntary statement.'

'Thanks for the tip! I don't mind telling you now that we
aren't through with that old goat. Not by a long way!'

'That's what I thought,' the Crab said dryly. 'Well, I'll go
back to the kitchen. The Shrimp needs that practice. Badly.
Goodbye.'

Ma Joong made his way through the shrubbery to the
veranda of the Red Pavilion. When he saw that Judge Dee
wasn't there, he sat down in the large armchair, put his feet up
on the balustrade, and contentedly closed his eyes. He fondly
tried to visualize Silver Fairy's many charms.

In the meantime Judge Dee had been interrogating the innkeeper on the history of the Red Pavilion.

The startled man scratched his head.

'As far as I know, sir,' he replied slowly, 'the Red Pavilion
is now exactly as it was fifteen years ago, when I bought this
hostel. But if Your Honour wishes any changes made, I shall
of course . . .'

'Isn't there somebody who was here before that time?' the
judge interrupted him. 'Say about thirty years ago?'

'Only the old father of the present doorkeeper, I think, sir. His son took over from him ten years ago because . . .'

'Take me to him,' Judge Dee snapped.

Muttering confused apologies the manager led him through the noisy servant quarters to a small yard. A frail old man with a ragged beard was sunning himself there, seated on a wooden box. Blinking at Judge Dee's shimmering robe of green brocade, he made to rise, but the judge said quickly:

'Remain seated, a person of your venerable age should not be bothered. I only want to know something about the history of the Red Pavilion, I am interested in old houses, you see. Do you remember when the bedstead in the Red Room was moved to the wall opposite?'

The greybeard tugged at his thin moustache. Shaking his head he answered:

'That bedstead was never moved, sir, no. At least, not in my time, that is. It was standing against the south wall, on your left when you enter. That's its proper place, and there it has been, always. I wouldn't speak for the last ten years, though. They may have changed it recently, they are always changing things, nowadays.'

'No, it's still there,' the judge reassured him. 'I am staying in those apartments now.'

'Fine rooms,' the old man mumbled, 'the best we have. And the wistaria ought to be in bloom now. I planted it myself, must be twenty-five years ago, about. Did a bit of gardening, too, in those days. Took the wistaria from the kiosk in the park, I did. They were breaking down the kiosk; a pity, it was fine old carpenter's work. They put up one of your modern buildings there, two stories, the higher the better! Transplanted trees there too. Spoiled the view from the veranda. You could watch beautiful sunsets from there, sir! See the pagoda of the Taoist temple against the evening sky. And those tall trees made the Red Pavilion damp, too, I'd say.'

'There's a thick shrubbery directly in front of the veranda,' Judge Dee remarked. 'Did you plant that too?'

'Never, sir! There oughtn't to be shrubbery close to a veranda, sir. If it isn't kept clean, it'll attract snakes and other vermin. The park guards planted those, the silly fools! I caught a couple of scorpions there; the guards are supposed to keep the place tidy, supposed, I say! I prefer an open, sunny place, sir, especially since I got this rheumatism. It came sudden-like, I said to my son, I said . . .'

'I am glad to see,' the judge interrupted hurriedly, 'that you are remarkably hale and hearty, for your age. And your son is looking after you well, I hear. Well, thanks very much!'

He walked back to the pavilion.

When he stepped out on the veranda Ma Joong hurriedly jumped up, and reported to him what the Crab had said about Wen's travelling plans.

'Of course Wen can't leave,' the judge said curtly. 'He is guilty of false testimony. Find out where he lives, we'll pay him a visit this afternoon. Now, go first to Kia's hostel, and tell the youngster that I want to see him, here and now. Then you can go and have your noon-rice. But see to it that you are back here in an hour or so. There's much to do.'

Judge Dee sat down near the balustrade. Slowly caressing his long sidewhiskers, he tried to reason out how the old gate-keeper's statement could be made to fit Tao Pan-te's story. The arrival of the young poet roused him from these cogitations.

Kia Yu-po looked very nervous; he made several bows in quick succession in front of the judge.

'Sit down, sit down!' Judge Dee said, irritated. When Kia had taken the bamboo chair, the judge sourly studied his dejected face. After a while he began suddenly:

'You don't look like a habitual gambler, Mr Kia. What made you try your luck at the gaming table? And with disastrous result too, I am told.'

The young poet looked embarrassed. After some hesitation he replied:

'I am really a quite worthless person, Your Honour! Except for a certain facility in making poetry, I have nothing to commend myself. I am much given to moods, always let myself drift along with the circumstances of the moment. As soon as I had entered that accursed gambling hall, the spirit of the place took hold of me, I . . . I simply couldn't stop! I can't help it, sir, it's just the way I am. . . .'

'Yet you are planning to pass the State examinations for entering upon an official career?'

'I had my name listed for the examinations only because two of my friends did, sir, I let myself be carried away by their enthusiasm! I know full well that I am not good enough for becoming an official; my only ambition is to live quietly somewhere up-country, read and write a little, and . . .' He paused, looked down at his restless hands, then went on unhappily: 'I feel terribly embarrassed towards Mr Feng, sir, he has such great expectations of me! He has been very kind to me, even wants me to marry his daughter . . . I feel all that kindness as . . . as a burden, sir!'

Judge Dee reflected that this young man was either utterly sincere or a consummate actor. He asked evenly:

'Why did you lie this morning in court?'

The youngster's face turned red. He stuttered:

'What . . . what does Your Honour mean? I . . .'

'I mean that you didn't enter the dressing-room by mistake, you went there expressly to inquire after Autumn Moon. Thereafter you were seen entering the path that leads to her private pavilion. Speak up, were you in love with her?'

'In love with that haughty, cruel woman? Heaven forbid, sir! I can't understand why Silver Fairy admires her so much, she often treated her and the other girls most harshly, whipping them at the slightest provocation! She even seemed to take pleasure in that, the repulsive creature! I wanted to make sure that she wasn't going to punish Silver Fairy for spilling wine on the robe of that wretched old curio-dealer, that's why I went after them, sir. But when I passed the Queen Flower's pavilion, all was dark there. So I went on and walked in the park for some time, to cool my head.

'I see. Well, here's the maid with my noon-rice. I'll have to change into a more comfortable dress.'

The poet hurriedly took his leave, mumbling excuses and looking even more dejected than before.

Judge Dee changed into a thin grey robe, then sat down to his meal. But he hardly tasted what he ate, his thoughts were elsewhere. After he had drunk his tea he got up and started to pace the veranda. Suddenly his face lit up. He stood still and muttered:

'That must be the solution! And that puts the death of the Academician in quite a different light!'

Ma Joong stepped out on the veranda. Judge Dee said briskly:

'Sit down! I have found out what happened to Tao's father, thirty years ago!'

Ma Joong sat down heavily. He was tired but happy. At the Widow Wang's he had found Silver Fairy much better, and while the widow was preparing the noon meal, he had done considerably more with the girl up in the attic than talk about their native place. In fact he had been so busily engaged that, when they went down at last, he had only had time for one quick bowl of noodles.

'Tao's father was indeed murdered,' the judge resumed, 'and in the sitting-room here.'

Ma Joong slowly digested that announcement. Then he protested:

'But Tao Pan-te stated that he had found the corpse in the Red Room, Your Honour!'

'Tao Pan-te was mistaken. I discovered that because he mentioned that the bedstead was on his right side, against the

94

north wall. I made inquiries and found that the bedstead of the Red Room has always been where it is now, on the south side, against the wall on the left. However, although the inside of these apartments has never been changed, thirty years ago the outside was entirely different. The wistaria that now partly screens this veranda was not yet there, neither were the park restaurant and the tall trees opposite. From this veranda one had an unobstructed view, and one could enjoy beautiful sunsets.'

'I suppose one could,' Ma Joong said. Silver Fairy was really a sweet girl. Knew what a man wanted, too.

'Don't you see it? The boy had never been here before, but he knew that the suite was called Red Pavilion because the bedroom was done all in red. When he entered the sitting-room it was bathed in the red glow of sunset! No wonder he mistook the sitting-room for the Red Room—which he had expected to see!'

Ma Joong looked over his shoulder at the sitting-room, taking in the sandalwood furniture, all left its natural colour. He nodded ponderously.

'Tao's father was killed in the sitting-room,' Judge Dee went on. 'It was there that his son saw his dead body, and got a glimpse of the murderer, clad in a white undergarment—not in a red robe, as the boy thought. As soon as the boy had rushed out, the murderer removed the body to the Red Room, locking the door behind him. He threw the key inside through the barred window, thus setting the stage for the alleged suicide. He assumed that nobody would pay attention to what the frightened young boy might say.' He paused a moment, then resumed: 'Since the murderer was clad in a white undergarment, I take it that he had a tryst with the courtesan, Green Jade, in the Red Room. Tao Kwang, his rival in love, surprised them, and he killed Tao with his dagger. Tao Pan-te's theory is right, his father was murdered. This throws a new light on the death of the Academician, Ma Joong. That was also a murder

95

staged as a suicide, in exactly the same manner as thirty years ago. The Academician was killed in the sitting-room, where anybody can enter freely and unobserved by way of this veranda. Then his body was brought to the Red Room, with his papers and everything. It worked once, so the murderer thought he might as well repeat the trick! And that constitutes an important clue to his identity!'

Ma Joong nodded slowly.

'That means that either Feng Dai or Wen Yuan is our man, sir. There's one important difference between the two cases, though. When the Academician was found dead, the key was not on the floor but inside the lock! You can't throw it into that position, sir. Not in ten thousand years!'

'If Feng is indeed our man, I could explain that point too,' the judge said pensively. 'In any case, I am certain that, if we identify the murderer of Tao Kwang and the Academician, we shall also know exactly what happened to the Queen Flower.' He frowned and added after some reflection: 'Yes, I'd better have a talk with Silver Fairy, before I see the curio-dealer. Do you know where we can find her?'

'In her dormitory behind the Crane Bower, Your Honour. She said she would go back there today.'

'Good. Take me there!'

# XI

Since it was still early in the afternoon, the street of the dormitories was quite busy. Messengers and tradesmen went in and out of the front doors, and everywhere one heard the sound of flutes, guitars and drums as the courtesans practised music and singing.

Ma Joong halted in front of the door marked 'Second Rank, No. 4'. He explained to the surly elderly woman who opened that they wanted to see the courtesan Silver Fairy, on official business. The woman silently led them to a small waiting-room, then went to fetch the girl.

Silver Fairy came in and made a low bow. She discreetly ignored the wink that Ma Joong gave her behind Judge Dee's back. The judge motioned the elder woman to leave them alone, then kindly addressed the girl:

'I am told that you are a pupil of the Queen Flower. She taught you singing and dancing, I suppose?' As the girl nodded, he went on: 'So that means that you came to know her well, doesn't it?'

'Oh yes, sir! I saw her nearly every day.'

'In that case you'll be able to enlighten me on a point that is puzzling me. I gathered that she had expected my colleague, Magistrate Lo, to buy her out, and I know that she was very disappointed when she found that she had been mistaken. Then she began at once to look for another patron. This proves clearly that she was keen to find a lover willing to take her away and marry her, doesn't it?'

'Very keen indeed, sir! She often told me and the other girls that being chosen Queen Flower is the golden chance for finding a wealthy protector and establishing yourself in a secure position for life.'

'Exactly. That being so, why then did she refuse the offer of such an eminent and wealthy person as the late Academician Lee Lien?'

'I have been wondering about that too, sir! I discussed it with the other girls; we all think that she must have had a special reason, but we can only guess what that was. There was something secretive about their relationship, we never knew where they ah . . . sported together. He invited her to all his parties, but after dinner they never made use of the private rooms provided by the restaurants. And she never went back with him to his own hostel either. After I had heard that the Academician had killed himself because of her, I . . .' She blushed and gave the judge a quick look. 'Well, I mean to say, I was a bit curious about how those two had gone about it, so I asked the old maidservant who looks after the Queen Flower. But she said that the Academician visited the Pavilion only once, on the same night that he committed suicide. And on that occasion they only had a brief talk. Of course the Queen Flower has the freedom of the island, so there are numerous other places where she can receive her lovers. Yesterday afternoon I made bold to ask her herself, but was told curtly to mind my own business. I thought that rather strange, for she always told us in great detail about her intimate experiences. I remember how she made all of us laugh when she described how that portly Magistrate Lo had . . .'

'Quite!' Judge Dee cut her short hastily. 'You are a good singer, I hear. According to my lieutenant you are studying under a certain Miss Ling, a former courtesan.'

'I didn't know that your man is so talkative!' the girl said, giving Ma Joong an annoyed look. 'If the other girls here get the wind of it, they'll engage Miss Ling too, and presently they'll all be singing the same songs as I!'

'We'll keep your secret!' the judge said with a smile. 'I want to have a talk with Miss Ling, you see, about the old days here. I don't want others to know about that interview, therefore I can't summon her officially. I leave it to you to arrange a suitable meeting place.'

'That would be difficult, sir,' she said with a frown. 'As a matter of fact, I went to see her just now. She wouldn't let me in, she said through the door that she was coughing badly again, and that she wouldn't be able to teach me for a week or so.'

'She can't be too ill to answer a few simple questions,' Judge Dee remarked testily. 'Go and warn her that in an hour or so you'll be coming back to her place, together with me.' He got up and added: 'I'll pass by here again later.'

Silver Fairy conducted them ceremoniously to the door. Outside the judge said to Ma Joong:

'I want Tao Pan-te to be present when I question Miss Ling, for he'll be able to make useful suggestions. Let's ask in that large wine shop over there where we can find him!'

They were in luck; the manager informed them that Tao Pan-te happened to be there. He was in the warehouse behind the shop, inspecting a newly arrived lot of winejars.

They found Tao bent over a large earthenware jar, sealed with clay. He apologized profusely for receiving them in a warehouse, and wanted to take them upstairs to sample the new wine. But Judge Dee said:

'I am in rather a hurry just now, Mr Tao. I only wanted to tell you that later in the afternoon I shall question an old woman who thirty years ago was a famous courtesan here. I thought you'd like to be present.'

'I certainly would!' Tao exclaimed. 'How did you find her, sir? I have been trying to locate such a person for years!'

'It seems that few people know about her existence. I am now going somewhere else, Mr Tao. On my way back I'll pick you up here.'

Tao Pan-te thanked the judge warmly.

When they were outside again Judge Dee remarked:

'It would seem that Mr Tao takes a much greater part in his business than he made me believe this morning!'

'Few people dislike a taste of a new brand!' Ma Joong said with a grin.

Wen Yuan's curio-shop was located on a busy corner. They found it crammed with larger and smaller tables loaded with vases, statues, lacquer boxes and other antiques of all kinds and sizes. When the shop assistant had gone upstairs with Judge Dee's large red visiting card, the judge whispered to Ma Joong:

'You'll go upstairs with me, I'll say you are a collector of porcelain.' He cut the tall fellow's protests short, saying: 'I want you to be there, as a witness.'

Wen Yuan came hurriedly down and welcomed the judge with a low bow. He started on the usual polite phrases but his thin lips were twitching, he could only bring out a confused stutter. Judge Dee said cordially:

'I had heard so much about your fine collection, Mr Wen, that I couldn't resist the temptation to come here and have a look.'

Wen again made an elaborate obeisance. When he had righted himself it was clear that, having learned the innocent object of Judge Dee's visit, he had got over his fright. He said with a deprecating smile:

'What I have here downstairs is nothing, Your Honour! These things are meant only for ignorant tourists from up-country. Allow me to lead you upstairs!'

The hall on the second floor was tastefully furnished with good antique pieces, and on the shelves along the walls stood a choice collection of porcelain. The curio-dealer took Judge Dee and Ma Joong to a small study at the back, and bade the judge sit down at the tea table. Ma Joong stood himself behind Judge Dee's chair. The screened light of the paper windows fell on the scroll paintings that covered the walls, showing to advantage their delicate colouring, mellowed by age. It was agreeably cool there, but Wen insisted on presenting his guest

100

with a beautiful silk fan. As the curio-dealer was filling Judge Dee's cup with fragrant jasmine tea, the judge said:

'I myself am interested in antique pictures and manuscripts. I brought my assistant along, because he is an expert on porcelain.'

'That's a lucky chance for me!' Wen said eagerly. He placed a square lacquer box on the table and took from its padded inside a slender white flower vase. He resumed: 'This morning a man brought this vase to me, but I have some doubts about it. Would the gentleman favour me with his opinion?'

The unhappy boxer stared at the vase with such a horrible scowl that Wen hastily put it back in the box, saying contritely:

'Yes, I too suspected it was a fake, but I hadn't thought it was as bad as all that. Well, the gentleman certainly knows porcelain!'

As Ma Joong resumed his position behind Judge Dee's chair with a suppressed sigh of relief, the judge addressed the curio-dealer affably:

'Sit down, Mr Wen! Let's have a leisurely talk.' As Wen took the seat opposite them the judge added casually: 'Not about antiques, but about the lies you told this morning in court.'

Wen's hollow face went sickly pale. He stammered:

'This person fails to see what Your Honour . . .'

'You stated,' Judge Dee interrupted coldly, 'that last night you came directly here from the Crane Bower. You thought that nobody had seen you cruelly maltreating a defenceless girl in the courtesans' training hall. But a maidservant watched you, and reported to me.'

Red blotches had appeared on Wen's face. He moistened his thin lips, then said:

'I didn't think it necessary to mention that, Your Honour. Those wayward girls need some punishment from time to time and . . .'

'It's you who shall be punished! For contempt of court, which means fifty lashes with the heavy whip! Subtract ten lashes for your advanced age, the rest'll still suffice to cripple you for life!'

Wen jumped up and knelt before the judge. Touching his forehead to the floor he begged for mercy.

'Rise!' the judge ordered. 'You shan't be flogged, because your head will be chopped off on the execution ground. You are implicated in a murder!'

'A murder?' Wen screamed. 'Never, Your Honour! Impossible. . . . What murder?'

'The murder of the Academician Lee Lien. Someone overheard your talk with him, ten days ago, on the morning he arrived here.'

Wen stared at the judge with wide eyes.

'Near the landing stage, under the trees, you bastard!' Ma Joong growled.

'But nobody was . .' Wen began, then caught up with himself and continued: 'That is to say . . .' He broke off, making a desperate effort to collect himself.

'Speak up, tell the truth!' Judge Dee barked.

'But . . . but if our conversation was overheard,' Wen wailed, 'then you must know that I did what I could to make the Academician see reason! That I told him it was sheer madness to try to get hold of Feng's daughter, that Feng would take a terrible revenge and that he . . .'

'Tell the complete story!' the judge interrupted. 'How it led up to murder!'

'That crook Feng must have slandered me! I had nothing to do with the Academician's death! It must have been Feng, he himself!' He took a deep breath, then went on in a calmer voice: 'I'll tell you exactly what happened, sir! At dawn the Academician's servant came to my shop here, I had just risen. He said that Lee, whom I had been expecting the night before, had been held up by a collision with another boat, and now was waiting for me on the landing stage. I knew his father, Dr Lee the Censor, I expected to do good business with the son. I thought that perhaps he . . .'

'Keep to what really happened!' Judge Dee ordered.

'But Lee didn't want to buy any antiques. He told me that he wanted me to help him arrange a secret meeting with Jade Ring, Feng Dai's daughter! He had met her when their boats collided. He had tried to persuade her to pass the night with him in his cabin, but she had refused. Now the fool's pride was hurt; he was determined to force her to comply with his wishes. I tried to explain to him that it was absolutely impossible, that she was a virtuous girl and that her father was a wealthy man, with great influence not only here but also . . .'

'I know that. Tell me how your hatred for Feng Dai made you change your mind!'

He saw Wen's haggard face twitch. His guess had been right. The curio-dealer wiped the perspiration from his forehead. He spoke dejectedly:

'The temptation was too strong for me, Your Honour! I made a terrible mistake. But Feng always treats me as . . . as an inferior, both in business and in . . . in private affairs. I thought, fool that I was, that this was an opportunity for humiliating Feng, deal him a severe blow, through his daughter. And should the plan miscarry, then all the blame would go to the Academician. So I told Lee I knew a way to force the girl to come to him and grant him her favours. If he would come to my house in the afternoon, we would discuss the details.'

The curio-dealer shot a quick look at Judge Dee's impassive face before he went on:

'Lee came. I told him that formerly a leading citizen here had killed himself, because the courtesan he loved had jilted him. That it was well known that Feng Dai had been the dead man's rival in love, and that there were rumours that Feng had murdered him. There must have been some truth in those

103

rumours, Your Honour! I swear that on the night the man died I saw Feng, slinking about behind the hostel where it happened! I am convinced that it was indeed Feng who had murdered that man, making it appear as if he had committed suicide.' He cleared his throat, then continued: 'I told Lee that Miss Feng knew of those rumours about her father. If the Academician would send her a message, telling her that he possessed irrefutable proof of her father's guilt, she would certainly come to him, for she is very fond of her father. Then he could do with her what he liked, for she would never dare to accuse him. That's all, I swear it, Your Honour! I don't know whether the Academician actually did send her such a message; I don't know whether, if he did, the girl really paid him a secret visit. I only know that, on the night Lee died, I saw Feng in the park, just behind the Red Pavilion. But I don't know anything about what happened there. Please believe me, Your Honour!'

Again he fell on his knees and knocked his forehead repeatedly on the floor.

'I shall verify every word you say,' Judge Dee spoke. 'I hope that you told the truth—for your sake! Now you'll write out a full confession, stating that you told the court a deliberate lie, that after Autumn Moon had whispered to you that you could find Silver Fairy bound naked to a pillar in the training hall and completely at your mercy, you went there, and when the girl refused to comply with your disgusting proposals you cruelly beat her across her hips with a long bamboo flute. Rise, and do as I told you!'

Wen hastily came to his feet. With trembling hands he took a sheet of paper from the drawer and spread it out on the table. But after he had moistened his writing brush he didn't seem to know how to begin.

'I'll dictate it!' Judge Dee snapped. 'Write! I, the undersigned, herewith confess that on the night of the 28th day of the seventh month . . .'

When the curio-dealer had finished, the judge told him to impress his seal and thumbmark on the document. Then he pushed it over to Ma Joong, who also added his thumbprint, as a witness.

Judge Dee rose, put the document in his sleeve and said curtly:

'Your trip to the capital is off. You are under house arrest until further notice.'

Then he descended the stairs, followed by Ma Joong.

# XII

When they were walking down the street Judge Dee said:

'I admit that I did the Crab and that other friend of yours an injustice. They supplied valuable information.'

'Yes, those two are all right. I must say, though, that half of the time I don't get what they are talking about—especially the Crab! As to Wen, sir, did you believe what that mean crook was telling us just now?'

'Partly. We took him by surprise, I assume that what he told about the Academician wanting to possess Miss Feng, and about the mean stratagem Wen suggested to him is quite true. It fits the Academician's proud and overbearing attitude, and also Wen's cowardly, nasty character. It also explains why Feng is so eager to marry his daughter to Kia Yu-po. The young poet depends completely upon Feng, he'll never dare to send his bride back to her father when he discovers she isn't a virgin any more.'

'So you are convinced that Lee did actually rape her, sir?'

'Of course. That was why Feng killed him. He made it appear as if the Academician had committed suicide, just as, thirty years ago, he concealed his murder of Tao Kwang.' Seeing Ma Joong's doubtful expression, he resumed quickly: 'It has to be Feng, Ma Joong! He had the motive and the opportunity. And I now fully agree with your two friends the Crab and the Shrimp that the Academician was not the type of man to kill himself because of unrequited love. Feng must have murdered him. Next to the opportunity and a compelling motive, he also had a method that had turned out to be foolproof thirty years ago. I regret that there is no alternative, for Feng made a very favourable impression on me. But if he is a murderer, I shall have to proceed against him.'

'Perhaps Feng'll then give us some clues to the death of Autumn Moon, sir!'

'I certainly need them! Our discoveries about the murder of Tao Kwang and the Academician don't bring us one step nearer to solving the Queen Flower's death. I am convinced that there's a connecting link somewhere, but I haven't the faintest idea where to look for it.'

'Just now you said, sir, that you believed what the old goat said about Lee and Jade Ring. What about the rest?'

'After Wen had told us about his advice to the Academician, I noticed that he succeeded in collecting his wits. I fear that he then realized that I had been bluffing. He couldn't change what he had told us already, but he then and there decided to leave it at that. I have a feeling that he spoke with the Academician also about other matters which he thought it better not to disclose. Well, we'll find out in due time, I am not yet through with him!'

Ma Joong nodded. They walked on in silence.

Tao Pan-te stood waiting for them in front of the wine shop. The three men went on together to Silver Fairy's dormitory.

It was she herself who opened the door. She said in a low voice:

'Miss Ling was ashamed to receive you in her miserable hovel, sir. She insisted that I brought her here, ill as she was. I smuggled her into the training hall, it's not being used at the moment.'

She quickly took them there. Next to the pillar by the back window a slight figure was sitting hunched up in an armchair. She was clad in a plain dress of faded brown cotton. Her grey, untidy hair hung down over her shoulders; her thickly veined hands were lying in her lap. When she heard them come in, she raised her head and turned her blind face in their direction.

The light of the paper window fell on the disfigured face. Deep pockmarks covered the hollow cheeks, which showed unhealthy red patches. The opaque eyes were strangely still.

Silver Fairy went quickly to her, followed by the judge and his two companions. Bending over the grey head she said softly:

'The magistrate has arrived, Miss Ling!'

She wanted to get up but Judge Dee quickly put his hand on her thin shoulder and said gently:

'Remain seated, please. You shouldn't have gone to all the trouble to come here, Miss Ling!'

'This person is completely at Your Honour's disposal,' the blind woman said.

Involuntarily the judge shrank back in incredulous horror. Never had he heard such a rich and warm, utterly lovely voice. Coming from that disfigured old woman, the voice seemed a cruel, outrageous mockery. He had to swallow a few times before he resumed:

'What was your professional name, Miss Ling?'

'I was called Gold Jasper, sir. People admired my singing and my . . . beauty. I was nineteen years old when I fell ill and . . .' Her voice trailed off.

'At that time,' Judge Dee continued, 'a courtesan called Green Jade was chosen Queen Flower. Did you know her well?'

'I did. But she died. Thirty years ago, during the epidemic. I was one of the first who caught the disease. I heard about Green Jade's death only several weeks afterwards, when I was . . . cured. She got the disease a few days after me. She died.'

'I suppose Green Jade had many admirers?'

'Yes, there were many. Most of them I didn't know. I knew only two well, both of this island, Feng Dai and Tao Kwang. When I had got better, Tao had died, and Green Jade had died.'

'Didn't Wen Yuan, the curio-dealer, also try to win her favour?'

'Wen Yuan? Yes, I knew him too. We avoided him; he liked to hurt women. I remember he gave Green Jade many costly presents, but she wouldn't even look at them. Is Wen still alive? If he is, he must be over sixty now. It's all so long ago.'

A group of courtesans passed by the window, talking excitedly. A peal of gay laughter rang out.

'Do you think,' Judge Dee asked again, 'that there was some truth in the rumour that Feng Dai was Green Jade's lover?'

'Feng was a handsome man, as I remember him. Straightforward and dependable. There wasn't much to choose between him and Tao Kwang, I think. Tao Kwang was also handsome, also a good, honest man. And also very much in love with her.'

'There were also rumours that Tao Kwang killed himself because she had preferred Feng. You knew him, Miss Ling. Do you think it likely that Tao Kwang would have done that?'

She didn't reply at once. She raised her blind face and listened to the guitar music that had started in a room upstairs. It was the same theme, repeated again and again. She said:

'She ought to tune her instrument better. Yes, Tao Kwang loved Green Jade deeply. Perhaps he did kill himself because of her.' Hearing Tao Pan-te's quick intake of breath, she asked:

'Who is that with you, sir?'

'One of my assistants.'

'It isn't true,' she said quietly. 'I heard him, he too must have known Tao Kwang well. He can tell you more about him than I, sir.'

Suddenly a violent attack of coughing racked her frame. She

took a crumpled handkerchief from her sleeve and wiped her lips. When she put it back it showed red stains.

Judge Dee realized that the woman was mortally ill. He waited till she had recovered, then resumed quickly:

'It was also said that Tao Kwang didn't commit suicide, but was killed by Feng Dai.'

She slowly shook her head.

'That's certainly slander, sir. Tao Kwang was Feng's best friend. I have heard them talk together—about Green Jade. I know that if Green Jade chose one of them, the other would have abided by her decision. But she didn't choose, I think.'

Judge Dee gave Tao Pan-te a questioning look. He shook his head. There seemed no point in asking more questions. Then the beautiful voice resumed:

'I think Green Jade wanted a man who was not only good-looking, and of a staunch character, and wealthy. She wanted more. A man who had all that, but also a wild, reckless strain. A man who would carelessly spend all he had, property, position, reputation—everything. Throw it away, casually, without even thinking about it. Because of the woman he loved.'

The voice ceased. Judge Dee stared fixedly at the window. The guitar theme, repeated with irritating insistence, was jarring on his nerves. With an effort he took hold of himself.

'I am most grateful, Miss Ling. You must be tired, I'll have a sedan chair called for you.'

'I appreciate your consideration. Thank you, sir.'

The words were obsequious, but the tone was that of a great courtesan, graciously dismissing an admirer. They gave the judge a sharp pang. He gave a sign to the others. They left the hall together.

Outside Tao Pan-te muttered:

'Only her voice is left. Strange . . . these shadows from the past. I'll have to think this over, sir. I beg to be excused.'

Judge Dee nodded, then said to Ma Joong:

' You get a sedan chair for Miss Ling, Ma Joong. Let it come to the back door here, and help Silver Fairy to get Miss Ling inside without attracting attention. I'll go and make one more call, then I shall return to the Red Pavilion. You'll find me there in an hour or so.'

# XIII

Ma Joong went to the shopping centre and rented one of the small sedan chairs waiting there, with four bearers. He paid them in advance and added a generous tip. They trotted cheerfully behind him as he walked to the back door of the dormitory. Silver Fairy stood waiting with Miss Ling in the yard.

The girl helped Miss Ling inside, then stared disconsolately after the sedan chair till it had disappeared round the corner. Seeing her sad look, Ma Joong said with an awkward grin:

'Cheer up, dear! You needn't worry about anything, you can leave all your problems safely to my boss. That's what I always do!'

'You would!' she snapped. She went inside, slamming the door shut in his face.

Ma Joong scratched his head. Perhaps she had a point there. He strolled to the main street, in a pensive mood.

When he saw over the heads of the crowd the impressive gatehouse of the brothel guild's office, he halted in his steps. For a while he watched the stream of busy people going in and out there, then sauntered on again. He was deep in thought, trying to reach a weighty decision. Suddenly he went back on his tracks, walked to the office and elbowed his way inside.

Scores of sweating men were crowding in front of the long counter, waving slips of red paper at the row of clerks, and shouting at the top of their voices. Those men were the touts and runners of the restaurants and tea houses, the red slips bore the names of the courtesans or prostitutes wanted by the guests in their respective establishments. As soon as one of them had succeeded in handing his slip to a clerk, the latter would thumb one of the ledgers in front of him. If the woman was free, he would enter the time and the name of the house in his ledger, then stamp the slip and hand it to one of the errand boys loitering by the door. The boy would deliver the slip to the dormitory where the woman lived, and in due time she would proceed to where she was wanted.

Ma Joong pushed the watchman guarding the wicket at the end of the counter unceremoniously aside. He went straight on to the back of the office, where the head clerk sat throned behind his large desk. He was an enormously fat man, with a round, smooth face. He looked haughtily at Ma Joong with lazy, heavy-lidded eyes.

Ma Joong pulled his official pass from his boot and threw it on the desk. After the fat man had studied the document carefully, he looked up with a smile and asked politely:

'What can I do for you, Mr Ma?'

'Help me with a simple business transaction, that's what you can do. I want to redeem a courtesan of the second rank, called Silver Fairy.'

The fat man pursed his lips. He gave Ma Joong an appraising look, then took a bulky ledger from his drawer. He leafed it through till he found the entry he wanted, and slowly read it. He cleared his throat importantly and said:

'We bought her cheap, one and a half gold bars. But she is a popular girl, and a good singer too. We gave her expensive dresses, the bills are all here. They add up to . . .' He groped for his abacus.

'Cut the cackle! You spent a good deal of money on her, and she brought in fifty times more than that, so I'll pay you the original price, and cash too.'

He took the package with the two gold bars he had inherited from his uncle Peng from his bosom, removed the wrappers and laid them on the desk.

The fat man stared at the two shining bars, slowly rubbing his double chin. He sadly reflected that he couldn't afford to antagonize an officer of the tribunal, the big boss Feng wouldn't like that. It was a great pity though, this rascal seemed eager enough. If he had been an outsider, he would doubtless have been willing to pay double the amount, and a generous tip. This was one of those unlucky days, his heartburn was worse too. He belched, then, with a deep sigh, detached a sheaf of sealed receipts from the register and handed them to Ma Joong. Then he laboriously counted out the change, twenty silver pieces. He lingered fondly over the last one.

'Wrap them up nicely—all of them!' the tall man ordered.

The clerk gave him a pained look. Slowly he wrapped up the silver in a piece of red paper.

Ma Joong put the package and the papers in his sleeve, and went out.

He thought he had made the right decision. There came a time when a man had to settle down, and what woman could one settle down with better than with a wench from one's own village? He could easily raise a family on the salary Judge Dee paid him, that was better than spending it all on wine and stray girls, as had been his wont. The only snag was that his colleagues Chiao Tai and Tao Gan would tease him no end. Well, let them! When those rascals had seen his girl, they would shut up quickly enough!

While he was rounding the corner of the street of the Hostel of Eternal Bliss, he saw the inviting red shop-sign of a wine house. He decided to offer himself a drink.

But when he had pulled the door-curtain aside, he saw that the noisy taproom was packed already with happy drinkers. There was only one empty place left, at the table in front of the window, where a melancholy-looking young man was sitting, staring moodily at an empty wine jug.

Ma Joong pushed his way among the tables and asked:

'Do you mind if I sit down here, Mr Kia?'

The youngster's face lit up.

'With pleasure!' Then his face fell again as he added: 'Sorry I can't offer you anything, my last coppers went with this last jug. Old Feng hasn't coughed up his promised loan yet.'

He spoke with a thick tongue. Ma Joong thought that the last jug must have been the last one of an impressive row. He said jovially:

'Share a jug with me!' He called a waiter and ordered a large jug. He paid for it, and filled their beakers.

'Here's to our luck!' He emptied his beaker in one long draught, and hastily refilled it. The poet followed his example, then said morosely:

'Thank you! I most certainly need luck!'

'You? Holy Heaven, man, you, the future son-in-law of Feng? Marrying the only daughter of the gambling boss—if that isn't the niftiest trick I have ever heard of for getting back your money from the tables!'

'That's just it! That's precisely why I need luck, baskets full of it, so as to get out of my troubles. And it's that swine Wen who landed me in this awful mess!'

'I still don't get what your troubles could be. But Wen is a son of a dog. I am with you there!'

Kia gave him a long look from his watery eyes. Then he said:

'Since the Academician is dead and gone, and the plan off, there's no harm in telling you, I suppose. Well, to cut a long story short, when I lost my money at that crooked table, that stuck-up Academician was sitting opposite me. Sanctimonious bastard said I played a reckless game! Afterwards he accosted me and asked whether I would like to get my money back, by earning it. I said, of course, yes, even if I would have to earn it. Then he took me to Wen's shop. They were concocting together some plot or other, against Feng Dai. Wen would get Feng into trouble, then Lee would use his influence in the capital to have Feng replaced by Wen as warden of this island. Lee wouldn't get any poorer by that, of course. That's high officials for you! Lee and Wen said they wanted me to worm myself into Feng's confidence, and act as their spy in Feng's mansion. I would have to conceal a small box in Feng's house, and that was all.'

'The dirty crooks! And you said yes, you fool?'

'No need to call me names, my man! Would *you* like to be marooned here on this island without a copper in your sleeve? Besides, I didn't know Feng, supposed he was as big a crook as the others, of course. And don't interrupt me, it's hard enough to keep to the thread of my sad narrative. By the way, didn't I hear you mention the word sharing in connection with this jug?' Ma Joong poured him out another beaker. The young poet drank greedily, and went on: 'All right, Lee said that I must go to see Feng and ask him for a loan, to be repaid after I had passed my examinations. It seems that Feng has a weak spot for young, talented poets in distress.

'So far so good. But when I went to see Feng I found him a decent, pleasant fellow. Agreed to let me have a loan, too. And he seemed to like me, for the next day he asked me for dinner, and again the next day. I met his daughter, a charming girl, and also Tao Pan-te, an excellent fellow. Fine judge of poetry too. Had read mine and said it had a touch of the antique elegance.'

Kia refilled his beaker, took a long draught and went on:

'After that second dinner I went to Wen, told him I refused to spy on Feng because I had found him a gentleman, and that, as a gentleman, I didn't spy on gentlemen. I added that, for precisely that reason, I wouldn't mind spying on him, on Lee, and all their friends. I may have added one or two things more, too. Well, Wen shouted that I wouldn't have got one copper from them anyway, because Lee had reconsidered and the whole plan was off. That suited me. I borrowed a silver piece from my landlord on the strength of Feng's promised loan, and betook myself to the centres of gaiety and frivolous pleasure. There I met a little girl, the loveliest and nicest I ever came across. The girl I had been waiting for all my young life.'

'Does she also make poetry?' Ma Joong asked suspiciously.

'Thank Heaven, no! Nice, simple, understanding girl! The restful kind, if you know what I mean. Stable. Heaven preserve me from literary girls!' He hiccoughed, then added: 'Literary girls are high-strung, and I am sufficiently high-strung myself. No sir, all the poetry that'll be done in my household shall be done by me. Exclusively!'

'Why are you sulking then?' Ma Joong shouted, 'August Heaven, some fellows have all the luck! You'll marry the Feng wench, and take the other girl, the restful one I mean, as concubine.'

Kia sat up in his chair. With an effort he focussed his eyes on his companion and said loftily:

'Feng Dai is a gentleman, and Miss Feng is not a wench but a well-educated, serious girl, although she is a bit high-strung. Feng likes me, she likes me, and I like them. Do you think I am such a cad as to accept Feng's only daughter and his money, then, as my modest contribution to the festivities, buy myself a courtesan and put her in the house?'

'I know lots of fellows who'd jump at the chance!' Ma Joong said wistfully. 'Including me myself!'

'I am glad I am not you!' Kia remarked nastily.

'Vice-versa!'

'Vice-versa?' the poet repeated slowly, creasing his forehead in a deep frown. Pointing with a crooked forefinger alternately at Ma Joong and himself he muttered: 'You . . . I . . . you . . . I.' Then he suddenly shouted: 'You are insulting me, sir!'

'Not at all!' Ma Joong said airily. 'You miscounted just now.'

'I apologize,' Kia said stiffly. 'I am greatly preoccupied with my sorrows.'

'Well, what are you going to do?'

'I don't know! If only I had the money, I'd buy that girl and vanish! I would then be doing Tao a favour too, he is fond of Miss Feng, you know, only he doesn't want to show it.' Bending over to Ma Joong he whispered hoarsely: 'Mr Tao has scruples, you see.'

Ma Joong heaved a deep sigh.

'Now you listen for once to an experienced man of the world, youngster!' he said disgustedly. 'You and Tao and all of you over-scrupulous brush-wielders only make simple things complicated for yourselves and for others. I'll tell you what to do. You marry the Feng girl, give her all you have got for one month, till she's as low-strung as a girl can get and implores you for a little respite. Then you say all right, she'll get her respite but you can't sweat it out either, so you buy yourself the restful wench and your wife'll be grateful and the other wench'll be grateful and they'll both be as restful or restive as you want them to be. Then you go out and buy yourself a third wife so that you can always propose a four-handed game of dominoes when they start making trouble, that's what my boss Judge Dee does with his three wives and he is a learned scholar and a great gentleman. And, since I mention my boss, I'd better be going now!'

He put the wine jug to his mouth and emptied it. 'Thanks for your company!' he said and walked off, leaving the indignant poet groping for a suitable reply.

## XIV

After Judge Dee had left the dormitory he had gone straight to Feng Dai's mansion. At the gate he gave his large official visiting card to the house steward. Soon Feng came rushing out into the front courtyard to meet the unexpected guest. He eagerly asked whether there had been any new developments.

'Yes,' the judge said evenly, 'Some new facts have come to light. Before taking official action, however, I would like to discuss these matters with you. And also with your daughter.'

Feng gave him a quick look. He said slowly:

'I take it that Your Honour desires the interview to be confidential?' When Judge Dee nodded, he continued: 'Allow me to conduct Your Honour to the garden pavilion where you spoke with Mr Tao this morning.'

He barked an order at the steward, then took the judge through the luxurious halls and corridors to the garden at the back of the mansion.

When the two men were seated at the small tea table, the steward poured out two cups, then withdrew. Soon the slender figure of Jade Ring came down the garden path. She was wearing the same black damask dress.

After Feng had introduced his daughter to the judge, she stood herself by the side of her father's chair, with modestly downcast eyes.

Judge Dee leaned back in his chair. Carefully smoothing down his long black beard, he said to Feng:

'I am informed that the Academician Lee Lien, having met your daughter when their boats collided, conceived dishonourable intentions regarding her. I am also informed that later he sent her a message, saying that if she didn't visit him in the

Red Pavilion he would make public certain facts regarding a crime allegedly committed formerly by you. Finally, that you were seen near the Red Pavilion on the night the Academician died. Do these allegations represent the truth?'

Feng had become very pale. He bit his lips, searching for words. Suddenly his daughter looked up and said calmly:

'Of course it's true. There's no use denying it, father, I had all along the feeling that it would come out.' Feng wanted to say something but she resumed quickly, looking the judge straight in the eye: 'This is what happened. On the night of the collision, the Academician insisted on apologizing to me personally. He spoke politely enough, but as soon as my maid had gone to fetch tea, he became offensive. He loaded me with fulsome praise, and said that, since our boats would be side by side all night, we might as well put that time to some good use. The man was so convinced of his own charm and importance that it hadn't occurred to him that I might refuse to sleep with him. When I did so, and in no uncertain terms, he flew into a terrible rage and swore he would possess me anyway, whether I liked it or not. I left him standing there and went into my cabin, barring the door on the inside. After I had come home I didn't tell my father, I was afraid that he would quarrel with the Academician and get himself into trouble. The whole incident wasn't worth that, the man had evidently been drunk.

'However, on the afternoon of the night he died, the miserable wretch sent me a message, of the tenor stated by you.'

Feng opened his mouth to speak but she laid her hand on his shoulder and went on:

'I love my father, sir, I'd do anything to help him. And there had indeed been rumours that once, many years ago, my father did something that might be explained in a manner detrimental to him. I slipped away that night and went to the Red Pavilion. I entered by the back entrance, unnoticed. Lee Lien was sitting at the table, writing something. He declared himself overjoyed that I had come, offered me a seat and said that he had known all along that Heaven had decided that I would be his. I tried to make him talk about my father's alleged crime, but he persistently evaded a direct answer. I said I knew that he had lied, that I was going back home and would tell my father everything. He jumped up, calling me awful names; he tore my robe down from my shoulders, hissing that he would have me then and there. I didn't dare to scream for help, for after all I had gone to his room secretly, and my reputation and that of my father would be ruined if people came to know about that. I thought I could keep him off. I fought back as well as I could, scratching his face and arms. He handled me most brutally. The proof is here.'

Disregarding her father's protests, she calmly loosened the bosom of her robe, let it drop down to her waist and showed the judge her bare torso. He saw the yellow and purple bruises on her shoulders, her left breast and both her upper arms. She pulled her robe over her shoulders again and resumed:

'During our struggle the papers on the table had been pushed aside, now I saw his dagger lying there. I feigned to give up my resistance. When he let my arms go to loosen my sash, I took the dagger and warned him that I would kill him if he didn't leave off. He wanted to grab me again, I struck out wildly with the dagger. Suddenly blood was spouting from his neck. He sank back into his chair, uttering a horrible, rattling sound.

'I was frantic. I ran home through the park and told my father everything. He'll tell you the rest.'

She made a perfunctory bow and rushed down the steps of the pavilion.

Judge Dee gave Feng a questioning look. The warden pulled at his side-whiskers, then he cleared his throat and began contritely:

'Well, I tried to calm down my daughter, sir, I explained to her that she was of course innocent of any crime, for it's a woman's good right to defend herself as well as she can when

121

she is being criminally assaulted. On the other hand, I said, it would be most awkward for both of us if the affair were dealt with publicly. It would affect her reputation, and although the rumours linking me with the old case are completely unfounded, I wouldn't like to see all that brought up again. Therefore I decided upon an ah . . . rather irregular line of action.'

He paused to take a sip from his tea. Then he went on in a firmer voice:

'I went to the Red Pavilion, where I found Lee dead in his chair in the sitting-room, as my daughter had described. There was little blood on the table and the floor, most of it was on his robe. I decided to make it appear as if he had committed suicide. I carried the body to the Red Room, laid it on the floor and placed the dagger in his right hand. Then I removed his papers from the table in the sitting-room to that in the Red Room, locked the door and left by the veranda. Since the only window the Red Room has is barred, I hoped that the Academician's death would be interpreted as a suicide. And so it was. The Queen Flower's statement about her having refused him supplied a convenient motive.'

'I suppose,' Judge Dee remarked, 'that you inserted the key into the lock after you had been called to investigate and after you had had the door broken open?'

'Indeed, sir. I had taken the key with me, for I knew that, after the body had been discovered, I would be the first to be notified. The manager came to me, we fetched Magistrate Lo, and went together to the Red Pavilion. After the door had been broken open, the magistrate and the constables went straight to the dead man, as I had expected. I quickly put the key inside the lock.'

'Quite,' the judge said. He thought for a while, tugging at his moustache. Then he said casually:

'In order to make your hoax perfect, you ought to have taken away that sheet with the Academician's last scribblings.'

'Why, Your Honour? Evidently the lecher was also desiring Autumn Moon!'

'No, he was not thinking of the Queen Flower, but of your daughter. The two circles represent rings of jade. When he had drawn those, it struck him that they resembled the full autumn moon, so he added, three times, those two words.'

Feng darted a quick look at the judge.

'Good heavens!' he exclaimed. 'That's true! Stupid of me not to think of that!' He added, embarrassed: 'I suppose that all this will have to come out now, and that the case will be reviewed?'

Judge Dee sipped his tea, his eye on the flowering oleander shrubs. Two butterflies fluttered about in the sunlight. The quiet garden seemed far removed from the noisy life of Paradise Island. Turning to his host, he said with a bleak smile:

'Your daughter is a courageous and resourceful girl, Mr Feng. Her statement, as amplified just now by you, would seem to solve the Academician's case. I am glad to know how he got those scratches on his arms, for those had made me believe for a moment that sinister forces had been at work in the Red Room. However, we still have the swellings in his neck. Your daughter didn't notice those?'

'No sir. Neither did I. Probably just a couple of swollen glands. As to the measures you propose to take regarding me and my daughter, sir, do you intend to . . .'

'The law says,' Judge Dee interrupted him, 'that a woman who kills the man who tries to rape her shall go free. But you tampered with the evidence, Mr Feng, and that is a serious offence. Before deciding upon a course of action, I want to know more about those old rumours your daughter referred to. Am I right in assuming that she meant the rumour that, thirty years ago, you killed Tao Pan-te's father Tao Kwang, because he was your rival in love?'

Feng sat up straight in his chair. He said gravely:

'Yes, Your Honour. It's needless to say that it's malicious slander. I did not kill Tao Kwang, my best friend. It's true that at the time I was deeply in love with the Queen Flower, the courtesan Green Jade. It was indeed my dearest wish to marry her. I was twenty-five at that time, and had just been appointed warden of the island. And my friend Tao Kwang, then twenty-nine, also loved her. He was married, but not too happily. However, the fact that we were both in love with Green Jade didn't influence our friendship. We had agreed that each would do his best to win her, and that the rejected candidate would bear the other no grudge. She, however, seemed reluctant to choose and kept putting off her decision.'

He hesitated, slowly rubbing his chin. Apparently he was debating with himself how he should go on. At last he spoke:

'I think I had better tell Your Honour the whole story. I ought to have spoken up thirty years ago, as a matter of fact. But I was a fool, and when I came to my senses, it was too late.' He heaved a deep sigh. 'Well, next to Tao Kwang and I, there was another suitor, namely the curio-dealer Wen Yuan. He tried to win her favour not because he loved her, but only because of his stupid need for self-assertion, he wanted to prove he was just as much a man of the world as me or Tao. He bribed one of Green Jade's maids to spy on her, suspecting that either I or Tao had already become her secret lover. Then, just at the time when Tao and I had decided we would insist that Green Jade make up her mind whom she preferred, Wen's spy told him that she was pregnant. Wen Yuan went at once with this information to Tao, and suggested to him that I was her secret lover and that Green Jade and I had been fooling him. Tao came rushing to my house. But he was a clever and just man, though a bit short-tempered, so it took me little time to convince him that I had had no intimate relations with her. We then discussed what we should do next. I wanted to go to her with Tao, tell her that we had discovered she loved another man and that we would therefore cease to bother her; that she had better say openly who that third person was, because we remained her friends, ready to help her, should she be in any difficulty.

'Tao didn't agree. He suspected that Green Jade had deliberately let us believe that she was hesitating between us two, so as to get more money out of us. I told Tao that such was not her character, but he would not listen and ran off. After he had gone I thought over the situation, and decided it was my duty to have another talk with Tao before he did something foolish. On the way to Tao's house I met Wen Yuan. He told me excitedly that he had just seen Tao and passed on to him the information that Green Jade was meeting her secret lover in the Red Pavilion that afternoon. He added that Tao had gone there already to find out who the man was. Fearing that Tao was about to fall into one of Wen's nasty traps, I rushed to the Red Pavilion, taking a short-cut through the park. When I had stepped up on the veranda, I saw the back of Tao's head as he was sitting in a chair, in the sitting-room. I called his name, and when he didn't move, I went inside. His breast was covered with blood, a dagger was sticking out from his throat. He was dead.'

Feng passed his hand over his face. Then he stared out into the garden with unseeing eyes. Taking hold of himself, he resumed:

'While I stood there, looking aghast at my friend's dead body, I suddenly heard footsteps approaching in the corridor. It flashed through my mind that, if I were found there, I would be suspected of having killed Tao, out of jealousy. I ran outside, to the Queen Flower's pavilion. But no one was there. Then I went home.

'As I was sitting in my library, still trying to sort out all possible explanations, a lieutenant of the magistrate came and summoned me, as warden, to the Red Pavilion. Someone had committed suicide there. I went and found the magistrate and his men in the Red Room. A waiter had seen Tao's body there, through the barred window. Since the door of the Red Room had been locked, the key lying on the floor, inside, the magistrate concluded that Tao had bled to death by a self-inflicted wound in his throat. A dagger was clasped in the dead man's hand.

'I didn't know what to do. After my flight from the Red Pavilion the murderer had evidently removed the corpse from the sitting-room to the Red Room, and thus set the stage for a suicide. The magistrate asked the hostel's manager about a possible motive, and he mentioned that Tao Kwang had been in love with the Queen Flower. The magistrate sent for her. She said that Tao Kwang had indeed been in love with her. Then she added, to my utter amazement, that he had offered to redeem her, but she had refused him. I frantically tried to catch her eye as she was standing there before the magistrate and delivering this utterly false statement, but she looked away. The magistrate decided then and there that it was a plain case of suicide because of unrequited love, and sent her away. I wanted to go after her, but he ordered me to stay. The smallpox epidemic was assuming alarming proportions in this region; that was also why the magistrate of Chin-hwa and his men were on the island. The whole night he kept me fully occupied with devising measures to prevent the disease from spreading; he wanted some of the buildings burned down, and other emergency measures taken. Thus I had no opportunity to go to Green Jade and ask for an explanation.

'I never saw her again. Early the next morning she had fled to the woods with the other girls, when the constables started to set fire to their dormitories. Out there she caught the disease, and she died. I only obtained her papers, which another girl had taken from her body before it was burned on the large communal pyre that had been lighted on the orders of the magistrate.'

Feng's face had acquired a deadly pallor, beads of perspiration had appeared on his brow. He groped for his tea cup and drank slowly. Then he continued in a tired voice:

'Of course I should then have informed the magistrate that Tao Kwang's suicide had been faked. It was my duty to have the murderer of my friend brought to justice. But I didn't know how far Green Jade had been implicated, and she was dead. And Wen Yuan had seen me going to the Red Pavilion. If I spoke up, Wen would accuse me of having murdered Tao Kwang. I was a miserable coward, I kept silent.

'Three weeks later, when the epidemic had been brought under control and life on the island was gradually returning to normal, Wen Yuan came to see me. He said he knew I had murdered Tao, and that I had arranged the faked suicide. If I did not cede my post of warden to him, he would accuse me in the tribunal. I told him to go ahead, I was glad that all would come out now, for my silence was weighing every day more heavily on me. But Wen is a sly scoundrel, he knew he had no proof, he had only tried to intimidate me. So he kept his peace, confining himself to spreading vague rumours hinting that I was responsible for Tao Kwang's death.

'Four years later, when I had succeeded in banishing Green Jade's memory from my mind, I married, and my daughter Jade Ring was born. After she had grown up she met Tao Kwang's son Tao Pan-te, and they seemed to like each other. It was my fond hope they would marry, some day. I felt that the union of our children would reaffirm the old friendship between me and Tao Kwang, my friend whose death I had failed to avenge. But the evil rumours spread by Wen Yuan must have reached Tao Pan-te's ears. I noticed a change in his attitude to me.' He broke off, and gave the judge an unhappy look. 'My daughter noticed the change in Tao too, for a long time she was very depressed. I tried to find another suitable bridegroom for her, but she would have none of the young men I mentioned to her. She is a very independent and headstrong girl, sir. That's why I was so pleased when she showed interest in

Kia Yu-po. I would have preferred a local man whom I knew better, but I couldn't bear to see my daughter unhappy any longer. And Tao Pan-te gave me clearly to understand that he had renounced her, by offering to act as middleman for her betrothal.'

He took a deep breath, then concluded:

'Now you know everything, sir. Including where I obtained the idea of making the Academician's death appear a suicide.'

Judge Dee nodded slowly.

As he refrained from making any comment, Feng said quietly:

'I swear by the memory of my dead father that what I told Your Honour about Tao Kwang's death is the complete truth.'

'The spirits of the dead are still among us, Mr Feng,' the judge reminded him gravely. 'Don't idly use their names.' After having taken a few sips from his tea, he went on: 'If you did indeed tell me the complete truth there must be a ruthless murderer about here. Thirty years ago he killed in the Red Pavilion the man who had discovered that he was Green Jade's secret lover. Last night he may have struck again there, this time at Autumn Moon.'

'But the coroner's report proved that she died from a heart attack, Your Honour!'

Judge Dee shook his head.

'I am not so sure about that. I don't believe in coincidences, Mr Feng, and the two cases resemble each other too closely. That unknown man got involved once with a Queen Flower, thirty years later he may well have become involved with another one.' Giving Feng Dai a sharp look, he added: 'And, speaking about Autumn Moon's demise, I have a feeling that you didn't tell me all you know about her, Mr Feng!'

The warden stared at him with what seemed genuine astonishment.

'The little I knew I told you, sir!' he exclaimed. 'The only aspect of her case I was reluctant to touch upon was her short-lived liaison with Magistrate Lo. But Your Honour discovered that yourself quickly enough!'

'I did indeed. Well, Mr Feng, I shall carefully consider what measures to take. That's all I am prepared to say now.'

He rose and let Feng conduct him to the gate.

# XV

Judge Dee found Ma Joong waiting for him on the veranda of the Red Pavilion. He said:

'I heard a very interesting story, Ma Joong. It would seem that the answer to all our problems lies in the past. Namely, in the murder of Tao Kwang, thirty years ago. We must go at once to see Miss Ling; she will supply a clue to the identity of the murderer of Tao Kwang. And then we shall also know who caused Autumn Moon's death. I shall . . .' He sniffed the air. 'There's a bad smell here!'

'I noticed it too. Probably some dead animal lying under the shrubs.'

'Let's go inside, I'll have to change.'

They went into the sitting-room. Ma Joong pulled the double doors closed. While he was helping the judge to put on a clean robe, he said:

'Before coming here I had a drink with that young poet Kia Yu-po, Your Honour. The Crab and the Shrimp were right, that old curio-dealer was indeed concocting with the Academician a plan to oust Feng Dai.'

'Sit down! I want to hear exactly what Kia said.'

After Ma Joong had finished, the judge remarked with satisfaction:

'So that was what Wen Yuan omitted to tell us! I told you that I had the distinct feeling that he was holding something back. Probably Wen and Lee had planned to put some seditious documents in the box Kia was to have smuggled into Feng's house. Then they would have denounced him to the authorities. But it doesn't matter much, for the plan was abandoned. Well, I just had a long talk with Feng and his daughter.

Apparently the Academician didn't commit suicide. He was killed.'

'Killed, Your Honour?'

'Yes. Listen to what those two told me.'

When he had given his lieutenant the gist of the conversation in the garden pavilion, Ma Joong said with grudging admiration:

'What a wench! That poet had the word for it, high-strung! I can see now why Kia isn't too eager to marry her. Marry her and you marry trouble! Lots of it! Well, so the case of the Academician is solved.'

The judge slowly shook his head.

'Not quite, Ma Joong. You have been in many a brawl. Tell me, do you think it likely that Jade Ring cut with a dagger in her right hand the right jugular vein of her attacker?'

Ma Joong pursed his lips.

'Likely, no. But not impossible, sir. When two persons are clinching with a drawn dagger in between, queer things happen, at times!'

'I see. I just wanted to check that point.' He thought for a while, then said: 'I think I'd better stay here, after all. I want to sort all this out so that I'll know exactly what to ask Miss Ling. You go and ask the Crab to take you to Miss Ling's hovel. Don't knock, just let the Crab point out the place to you. Then you come back to fetch me, and we'll go there together.'

'We could easily find the place by ourselves, Your Honour. I know it's somewhere on the waterside, opposite the landing stage.'

'No, I don't want to walk around there asking after Miss Ling. There may be a murderer about here, and Miss Ling is probably the only person who can supply information about him. I won't endanger her safety. Take your time, I'll wait for you here. I have plenty to think about!'

So speaking, he took off his outer robe again, laid his cap on

131

the table and stretched himself out on the couch. Ma Joong pushed the tea-table nearer so that the judge could easily reach it, then took his leave.

Ma Joong went straight to the large gambling hall. He thought that, since it was already late in the afternoon, the Crab and the Shrimp would have come back from their day-sleep at home. He found them indeed upstairs, watching the gaming tables with solemn faces.

He told them what he wanted, adding: 'Perhaps one of you could take me there?'

'We'll go together,' the Crab said: 'Me and the Shrimp are a team, you see.'

'We just came from there,' the Shrimp remarked, 'but a little exercise'll do us good, won't it, Crab? And my son'll be back from the river, maybe. I shall speak to the superintendent about our replacements.'

The small hunchback went downstairs and the Crab took Ma Joong to the balcony. When they had drunk several cups there, the Shrimp came back and said he had arranged that two of their colleagues would replace them for an hour or so.

The three men made their way through the busy streets, keeping to a westerly direction. Soon they were walking through the quiet alleys of the quarter of the street-vendors and coolies. When they came out on a piece of waste land, covered by thick undergrowth, Ma Joong remarked dubiously:

'You didn't choose a very cheerful neighbourhood to live!'

The Crab pointed at the cluster of tall trees over on the other side.

'Beyond those,' he said, 'you'll find it quite pleasant. Miss Ling lives there in her small shed, under a large yew-tree. And our house is farther on, among the willows on the waterside. This waste land may not be cheerful, but it separates us from the noisy streets.'

'At home, we like it quiet,' the Shrimp added.

The Crab, who was walking ahead, entered the narrow path

leading through the trees. Suddenly there were the sounds of breaking branches. Two men leaped from the undergrowth. One grabbed the Crab's arms, the other gave him a fearful blow with a knobstick in his heart region. He wanted to raise his stick to brain the Crab, but Ma Joong sprang forward and placed a vicious fistblow on his jaw. As the ruffian slid to the ground, together with the groaning Crab, Ma Joong turned to the second rogue, but he had drawn a long sword. Ma Joong stepped back, just in time to avoid the thrust aimed at his breast. At that moment four other ruffians appeared; three had swords ready in their hands, the fourth raised the short spear he carried and shouted:

'Surround them and cut'm down!'

It flashed through Ma Joong's mind that it wasn't a very nice situation. His best chance was to try and wrench the spear from that tall scoundrel. But he must first get the small hunchback out of this, for he was not too sure that, even with the spear, he would be able to hold out for long against four swordsmen. He placed an accurate kick on the shaft of the spear aimed at him, but the tall ruffian held on to it. Ma Joong barked over his shoulder at the Shrimp:

'Run for help!'

'Get out of my way!' the hunchback hissed behind him. The small fellow brushed by Ma Joong's legs and went straight at the rogue with the spear. He poised his spear at the hunchback with an evil grin. Ma Joong wanted to spring forward to drag the Shrimp back, but the swordsmen closed in on him, leaving the hunchback to their leader. Just as Ma Joong dodged a swordblow at his head he saw that the Shrimp's hands had shot out, each swung an egg-sized iron ball attached to a thin chain. The spear wielder was falling back, trying frantically to ward off with his weapon the iron balls that came whirling towards him. Ma Joong's attackers now turned round to help their leader. But the Shrimp seemed to have his eyes everywhere at the same time, he swung round and let one of the iron balls bash in the skull of the nearest swordsman. He turned again, now the other ball crushed the shoulder of the leader. The others tried to stab the hunchback, but he gave them no chance. He was dancing around with incredible speed, his small feet seemed hardly to touch the ground, his grey hair fluttering in the breeze. And all around him were the whirling iron balls, a deadly, impenetrable curtain.

Ma Joong stepped back and watched breathlessly. This was the secret art of chain-fighting which people spoke about sometimes, in hushed voices. The chains were lashed to the Shrimp's thin forearms with leather straps, he controlled their length by letting them slip through his hands. He crushed the arm of the second swordsman with the shortened chain in his left hand, then let the right iron ball shoot out to the chain's full length. It smashed the face of the third hooligan with the force of a sledgehammer.

Only two of the attackers were still on their feet. One made a futile attempt to catch the left ball on his sword, the other turned to make his escape. Ma Joong wanted to jump the latter, but it wasn't necessary. The Shrimp let the right iron ball hit his spine with a sickening thud, the man fell forward flat on his face. At the same time the left chain had slung itself round the sword of the last rogue that remained; it curled upwards along the blade like an angry snake. The Shrimp jerked the man closer, shortened the chain in his other hand, and let the iron ball smash his temple. It was all over.

The small hunchback skilfully caught one ball in each hand, slung the chains round his forearms and pulled his sleeves down over them. When Ma Joong stepped up to him he suddenly heard a deep voice behind him saying sadly:

'You twisted again!'

It was the Crab. He had freed himself of the limp body of the club-wielder lying half over him and was sitting up now, with his back against a tree trunk. He repeated disgustedly: 'Twisted again!'

A CHAIN-FIGHTER DEFEATS THE ASSASSINS

The Shrimp turned on him and said sharply:

'I did not!'

'You did!' the Crab said firmly. 'I saw you use your elbow, clearly. It spoiled your last short-chain.' He rubbed his bulging chest, the blow that would have killed any other man didn't seem to have hurt him much. He scrambled up, spat on the ground and went on: 'Twisting is bad. It must be flip. From the wrist.'

'A twist gets you in sideways!' the Shrimp said crossly.

'It must be a flip,' the Crab said stolidly. He bent over the club-wielder and muttered: 'Pity I nipped his throat a bit too hard.' He went on to the leader, the only ruffian who was still alive. He was lying there gasping, his hands pressed to the left side of his breast that was oozing with blood. 'Who sent you?' the Crab asked.

'We . . . Lee said . . .'

The man's voice was stifled by a stream of blood that came gushing from his mouth. His body twitched convulsively, then he lay still.

Ma Joong had been examining the other dead men. He said with undisguised admiration:

'Mighty fine work, Shrimp! Where did you learn that?'

'I trained him,' the Crab said quietly. 'Ten years on end. Keep him at it, daily. Well, we are near our home here, let's go and have a drink. We can gather up the remains later.'

They walked on, the Shrimp lagging behind, still sulking. Ma Joong asked the Crab wistfully:

'Couldn't I learn that too, Crab?'

'No. Hefty fellows like you and me can't. We'd always want to impart our force to those balls, and that's wrong. You just set them into motion, thereafter you must let them do the work, you only guide them. Technically that's called the suspended balance, for you are hanging, as it were, between those two whirling balls, you see. Only small, light fellows can do that. Anyway, you can use this art only out in the open, with

136

plenty of elbow space. I do all the indoor fighting, the Shrimp does the outside work. We are a team, you know.' Pointing at a sagging small shed of cracked boards leaning against a tall yew tree, he remarked casually: 'That there is Miss Ling's place.'

A short walk brought them to the waterside, lined by willow trees. A small, white-plastered house with a thatched roof stood behind a rustic bamboo fence. The Crab took Ma Joong round the house to the well-kept garden, covered with pumpkin plants, and made him sit down on the wooden bench under the eaves. From there one had a good view of the broad expanse of water beyond the willow trees. Surveying the peaceful surroundings, Ma Joong's eye fell on a high bamboo rack. Six pumpkins were displayed on it, each at a different height above the ground.

'What is that for?' he asked curiously.

The Crab turned to the Shrimp, who was coming round the house, still looking sour. He snapped at him:

'Number three!'

Quick as lightning the right hand of the small hunchback shot out. There was a clanking of iron, then the ball smashed the third pumpkin on the rack.

The Crab rose ponderously, picked the half-crushed pumpkin up and laid it on the palm of his large hand. The Shrimp stepped up to him eagerly. Silently the pair examined the pumpkin. The Crab shook his head and threw it away. He said with a reproachful look:

'Just as I feared! Twisted again!'

The small man grew red in the face. He asked indignantly:

'Do you call half an inch out of centre a twist?'

'It isn't a bad twist,' the Crab conceded. 'But still a twist. You use your elbow. It must be a flip. From the wrist.'

The Shrimp sniffed. After a casual look at the river, he said: 'My son won't be in for some time. I'll fetch a drink.'

He went into the house, and the Crab and Ma Joong walked

back to the porch. As Ma Joong resumed his seat, he exclaimed: 'So, you use them for target practice!'

'What else did you think we are growing pumpkins for? Every other day I set up six for him, different size, different position.' He looked over his shoulder to make sure that the Shrimp was out of earshot, then whispered gruffly at Ma Joong's ear: 'He is good. Very good. But if I say so he'll get slack. Especially on his short-chain work. I am responsible for him. He is my friend, you see.'

Ma Joong nodded. After a while, he asked:

'What does his son do?'

'Nothing much, as far as I know,' the Crab replied slowly. 'He's dead, you see. Fine, strapping lad, the Shrimp's son was. The Shrimp was proud of him, proud as the devil. Well, four years ago, the boy went out to fish, with the Shrimp's wife. Collided with a war-junk midstream, and they drowned. Both of them. Then the Shrimp would begin to blubber every time you mentioned his son. You can't work with a man like that, can you? I got fed up, and I said: 'Shrimp, your son isn't dead. Only you don't see him so often nowadays, because he's out on the river, mostly.' The Shrimp took that. I didn't say anything about his wife, mind you, because there's a limit to what the Shrimp takes from me. She had an awfully sharp tongue, anyway.' The Crab heaved a sigh. He scratched his head and went on: 'Then I said to the Shrimp: 'Let's ask for the night-shift, that'll give us a chance to meet your son when he comes back, in the afternoon.' And the Shrimp took that too.' Shrugging his broad shoulders, the Crab concluded: 'The boy won't come back no more, of course, but it gives the Shrimp something to look forward to, so to speak. And I can talk to him about his son now and then, without him beginning to sniffle.'

The Shrimp came outside with a large wine jar and three earthenware cups. He put them on the brightly scoured table-top, then sat down also. They drank a toast to the successful

138

fight. Ma Joong smacked his lips and let the Crab refill his cup. Then he asked:

'Did you know those bastards?'

'Two. They belong to a band of rogues from over the river. Fortnight ago they tried to hold up one of Feng's messengers. I and a colleague of mine were escorting him, and we killed three. The two who escaped then we got now.'

'Who is that fellow Lee the dying man blabbed about?' Ma Joong asked again.

'How many people of the surname Lee do we have on the island?' the Crab asked the Shrimp.

'Couple of hundred.'

'You heard him,' the Crab said, fixing Ma Joong with his protruding eyes. 'Couple of hundred.'

'Doesn't get us very far,' Ma Joong observed.

'Didn't get them very far either,' the Crab said dryly. And, to the Shrimp: 'The river looks good at dusk. Pity we aren't here more often, at night.'

'It's peaceful!' the Shrimp said contentedly.

'Not always, though!' Ma Joong remarked as he got up. 'Well, I suppose you fellows'll look into the affair we had out there. I must go back to my boss and report that I know where to find Miss Ling.'

'If you find her,' the Crab said. 'When we passed by there before dawn this morning, I saw a light there.'

'She being blind, a light means visitors,' the Shrimp added.

Ma Joong thanked them for their hospitality, then walked back through the gathering dusk. He paused a moment in front of Miss Ling's hovel. There was no light; it seemed completely deserted. He pulled the door open and cast a quick look at the semi-dark room that contained only a bamboo couch. No one was there.

## XVI

Back in the Red Pavilion Ma Joong found Judge Dee standing at the balustrade of the veranda, watching the park guards
who were lighting the coloured lampions among the trees. He
told the judge what had happened, and concluded:

'The net result is that I know exactly where Miss Ling lives.
But she isn't there, so we needn't go. At least not now. Probably her visitors took her out somewhere.'

'But she is very ill!' Judge Dee exclaimed. 'I don't like the
idea of her having visitors, I thought nobody knew about her
except your two friends and that girl Silver Fairy.' He tugged
worriedly at his moustache. 'Are you sure that the Crab and
the Shrimp were the intended victims of that murderous
attack, and not you?'

'Of course it was they, Your Honour! How could the
bastards have known I would be there? They were lying in
ambush for the Crab to avenge three of their gang, killed by
him during a hold-up two weeks ago. They didn't know about
the Shrimp!'

'If that were true, the hooligans must have been aware of
the fact that your two friends have the habit of sleeping during the day and not returning home until dawn. If you hadn't
happened to ask them to take you to Miss Ling's hovel, the
attackers would have been waiting there the entire evening
and night!'

Ma Joong shrugged his shoulders.

'Perhaps they were prepared for that!'

Judge Dee thought for a while, staring at the park restaurant opposite, where again a feast seemed to be in full swing.
He turned round and remarked with a sigh:

'I spoke rashly indeed when I said yesterday that I would

spend only one more day on Magistrate Lo's business! Well, I won't need you tonight, Ma Joong. You'd better go now and have your dinner, then amuse yourself a bit. Tomorrow morning we'll meet here again after breakfast.'

After Ma Joong had taken his leave, Judge Dee started to pace the veranda, his hands clasped behind his back. He felt restless, he didn't relish the idea of having his dinner alone in his room. He went inside and changed into a gown of plain blue cotton. Putting a small black skull-cap on his head, he left the Hostel of Eternal Bliss by the main gate.

Passing the front door of the inn where Kia Yu-po was staying, he halted in his steps. He might invite the young poet to share the evening meal with him and ask him more about Wen's scheme against warden Feng. Why would the Academician have given up that plot so suddenly? Had he perhaps decided that forcing Miss Feng to marry him was the easier way to get Feng's wealth into his hands, and without the need of letting the curio-dealer share it?

He went inside. But the manager informed him that the poet had left after the noon-meal, and not come back. 'And the other day I let him borrow a silver piece from me!' he added sadly.

The judge left the innkeeper to his worries and entered the first restaurant he saw. He ate a simple meal, then had his tea on the balcony upstairs. Sitting close to the balustrade, he aimlessly watched the crowd in the street below. On the corner a group of youngsters were adding more bowls of food to the altar of the dead erected there. Judge Dee counted on his fingers. The next day would be the thirtieth of the seventh moon, the end of the Festival of the Dead. Then the paper models and the other offerings would be burned. This entire night the gates of the Other World would still be open.

Leaning back in his chair, he vexedly bit his lips. He had been confronted with baffling problems before, but then there had been at least sufficient data for formulating some theories

141

and selecting some possible suspects. But he could not make head nor tail of the present situation. Doubtless one and the same criminal was responsible for' the thirty-year-old murder of Tao Kwang, and the demise of Autumn Moon. And had that man now also eliminated Miss Ling? He frowned worriedly. He could not get rid of the feeling that there was a connection between her disappearance and the attack on Ma Joong and his two friends. And the only clue he had was that the unknown murderer must be about fifty years old, and a man living on, or closely connected with, Paradise Island. Even the case of the Academician had not been completely cleared up. Jade Ring's story about how she killed him seemed straightforward enough, but his relationship to Autumn Moon remained a mystery. It was passing strange that nobody seemed to know where their intimate meetings had taken place. There must have been more to their relationship than mere amorous dalliance. It is true that he had planned to redeem the Queen Flower. But didn't his preoccupation with Jade Ring prove that it was some ulterior reason rather than ordinary passion that had made him decide to buy Autumn Moon out? Was she perhaps blackmailing him? He shook his head disconsolately. Since both the Academician and the Queen Flower were dead, he could never solve that mystery.

Suddenly he started to mutter angrily at himself. He had made a big mistake! The guests at the table next to him looked curiously at that tall, bearded gentleman who seemed to be working himself up into a rage all by himself. But Judge Dee didn't notice it. He rose abruptly, paid his bill and went downstairs.

He passed Kia Yu-po's hostel and walked along the bamboo fence on its left till he came to a small gate. It was standing ajar, on the jamb hung a wooden tablet, marked 'Private'.

He pushed it open and followed a well-kept path, winding among the tall trees. Their thick foliage screened off the noise from the street. When he had come out on the bank of a large pond, it was curiously still. A gracefully curved bridge of red-lacquered wood led across. While walking over the creaking boards he heard the splashes of the frightened frogs, jumping into the dark water.

On the other side a steep staircase led up to an elegant pavilion, raised about five feet above the ground on thick wooden pillars. It had but one floor, the pointed roof was decked with copper tiles, grown green with age.

Judge Dee went up on the balcony. After a quick look at the solid front door he walked round the pavilion. It had an octagonal shape. Standing at the balustrade at the back, he overlooked the garden behind Kia's inn and the side garden of the Hostel of Eternal Bliss beyond, dimly lit by the light coming from the park. He could vaguely discern the path leading to the veranda of the Red Pavilion. Turning round he inspected the back door. A strip of white paper had been pasted over the brass padlock, with the impression of Feng's seal on it. The door looked less solid than the one in front. As soon as he had put his shoulder against it, it burst open.

He stepped into the dark hall and, by groping located a candle on the side-table. He lighted it with the tinderbox that was lying beside it.

Raising the candle high, he surveyed the luxuriously appointed entrance hall, then had a quick look in the small sitting-room on the right. On the left of the hall he found a side-room, furnished only with a bamboo couch and a rickety bamboo table. Behind it was a washroom and a small kitchen. Evidently these were the maid's quarters.

He went out and entered the large bedroom opposite. Against the back wall he saw a huge bedstead of carved ebony, screened by gaudy curtains of embroidered silk. In front stood a round table of intricately carved rosewood, inlaid with mother of pearl. It could be used both for taking tea and for cosy dinners for two. The scent of a strong perfume lingered in the air.

The judge went over to the large dressing-table in the corner.

He looked casually at the round mirror of polished silver and the impressive array of pots and boxes of coloured porcelain where the dead woman had kept her powders and ointments, then inspected the copper padlocks of the three drawers. It was there that the Queen Flower would have stored away her notes and letters.

The padlock of the upper drawer had not been closed. He pulled it out but saw nothing but crumpled up handkerchiefs and greasy hairpins which gave off a bad smell. He hastily pushed it shut and went on to the next. The padlock of this one also hung loosely on the hinge. The drawer contained the articles a courtesan uses for her intimate toilet. He slammed it shut. The third drawer was securely locked, but when he jerked at the padlock the thin wood round the hinges that held it splintered away. He nodded with satisfaction. The drawer was stuffed with letters, visiting cards, used and unused envelopes, receipted bills and sheets of blank writing paper, some crumpled up, others soiled by greasy fingers and lip salve. Evidently the courtesan had not been a very tidy person. He took this drawer over to the table and emptied its contents there. He pulled up a chair and started to sort the papers out.

His hunch might prove entirely wrong, but he had to verify it. During the dinner in the Crane Bower the Queen Flower had casually mentioned that the Academician had given her a vial of perfume as a parting present, enclosed in an envelope. She had asked him what perfume it was, but he had answered 'See that it reaches its destination'. Preoccupied with her thoughts about the perfume, she might well have paid no attention to something else he had said just before that, and remembered only his last words, which she had taken to be a jocular reference to the vial of perfume. But his words sounded like an instruction rather than an answer to her question. An instruction regarding another enclosure he had put in the envelope, next to the vial. Perhaps a message or a letter which the Academician wanted her to deliver to a third person.

He carelessly threw opened letters and visiting cards on the floor. He was looking for an unopened envelope. Then he found it. He leaned forward and held it close to the candle. The envelope was rather heavy, it bore no address, but was inscribed with a poem, in a strong, impressive calligraphy. It was a quatrain, reading:

> I leave with you this futile gift of floating fragrance,
> As floating as the sweet but futile dreams you gave to me,
> With this last dream: that in idle hours of remembrance,
> This scent may linger there where fain my lips would be.

The judge pushed his skull-cap back, pulled a hairneedle from his topknot, and slit the envelope carefully open with it. He shook out a flat vial of carved green jade with an ivory stopper. Then he eagerly took up the second, smaller envelope that fell out. It was securely sealed, and addressed, again in the Academician's handwriting: 'To His Excellency Lee Wei-djing, Doctor of Literature, former Imperial Censor, etc. etc., for his gracious inspection'.

He cut it open and found one sheet of note paper. It was a brief letter, written in excellent, concise literary style.

> To the Honoured Father: Your ignorant and unworthy son finds he can never emulate your indomitable courage and iron will-power, he dares not face the future. Having reached what now shall remain the peak of his career, he must leave off here. He has informed Wen Yuan that he cannot continue, entrusting him with taking appropriate measures.
>
> Not daring to come under your stern eyes, I write this letter to be transmitted to its high destination by the courtesan Autumn Moon. The sight of her exquisite beauty brightened my last days.
>
> On the 25th day of the seventh moon, during the Festival

of the Dead, the unworthy son, Lien, kneels down and three times touches his forehead to the floor.

Judge Dee sat back with a perplexed frown. The style was so terse that it was not easy to grasp the writer's exact meaning.

The first paragraph suggested that the retired Censor Lee, his son the Academician, and the curio-dealer Wen Yuan had been engaged together in some nefarious scheme, but that the Academician had at the last moment found that he lacked the courage and will-power to go through with it; and that he, unable to follow his father's instructions, saw suicide as the only solution. But that meant that the scheme involved much more than a petty plot of ousting a warden on a trumped-up charge! Heaven knows what weighty issues were at stake, matters of life and death, perhaps even affairs of state! He must again question that rascally curio-dealer, if necessary with legal severities, then visit the Academician's father. He must...

He wiped the perspiration from his forehead, it was stifling hot in the room, and the smoking candle smelled badly. He recollected himself. He must not go too fast, he must first try to reconstruct the sequence of events. When the Academician had reached his decision and handed the envelope to the Queen Flower, he did not commit suicide after all, because, before he could kill himself, he was killed by the girl he tried to rape. The judge hit his fist on the table. This was sheer nonsense! A man determined to end his life, trying to rape a girl! He refused to believe that such a thing was possible!

Yet the letter could not be a fake. And that the Academician had indeed decided to abandon a scheme was proved by Kia Yu-po's statement made to Ma Joong. Also Autumn Moon's not delivering the letter entrusted to her was quite in character. Whatever her relationship to the Academician might have been, as soon as he was dead the woman had become preoccupied by her next conquest, namely that of his gay colleague Lo. She had thrown the envelope unopened into her drawer and forgotten all about it. Until that night at the dinner, when Lo's defection had made her regret her dead admirer. Some facts fitted, others not. He folded his arms in his wide sleeves. Knitting his bushy eyebrows in a deep frown, he stared at the luxurious bedstead where the Queen Flowers of succeeding years had disported themselves with their chosen lovers.

Again he went over in his mind what he knew about the persons concerned in the three deaths that had taken place in that other bedroom, in the Red Pavilion. He tried to recall, in the exact words, what Feng Dai and his daughter Jade Ring had said. Also Wen Yuan's partial confession, and the additional information gathered by Ma Joong. Apart from the improbability of the Academician's wanting to rape a girl on the eve of his intended suicide, the circumstances of his death had been satisfactorily explained. After Miss Feng had accidentally killed him, her father had staged the faked suicide. The scratches on the hands and face of the Academician had been caused by Miss Feng, only the swellings on his neck remained unexplained. As regards Autumn Moon's death, her scratches had been caused by Silver Fairy when she tried to ward off the Queen Flower's vicious slaps. In her case the feature still unaccounted for was the blue bruises on her throat. He had a vague feeling that if he could connect those two unexplained facts, the riddle of the Red Room would be solved.

Then he suddenly saw a possible explanation. He jumped up and began to pace the floor. After a long while he stood still in front of the huge bedstead. Yes, he now saw the pattern! Everything had found its logical explanation, including the attempted rape, and the attack by the armed ruffians on Ma Joong! The secret of the Red Pavilion was unspeakably repulsive, even more horrible than his weird nightmare there, after he had discovered the white, naked body of the courtesan on the red rug! He suddenly shivered.

The judge left the Queen Flower's pavilion and went straight to the Hostel of Eternal Bliss. Standing at the counter he gave one of his red visiting cards to the manager, ordering him to have it taken immediately to the warden's residence, with the message that the Assessor wanted to see Feng Dai and his daughter as soon as possible.

When he was back in the Red Pavilion, Judge Dee went out on the veranda. Leaning over the balustrade he carefully scrutinized the shrubbery and undergrowth below.

Then he stepped back into the sitting-room and pulled the double door shut. After he had put the cross-bar into place, he also closed the shutters of the window. As he sat down at the tea-table he realized that it would become very hot in the closed room. But he could not afford to take any chances. He knew now that he was dealing with a desperate, completely ruthless murderer.

# XVII

Ma Joong had treated himself to a good dinner in a noodle rest-aurant, finishing two large jugs of strong wine. Now he was walking down the street of the dormitories, humming a gay tune. He was in a festive mood.

The elderly woman who opened the door marked 'Second rank, No. 4' gave him a sour look. She asked:

'What do you want *now*?'

'To see the courtesan Silver Fairy.'

Taking him to the staircase, the woman asked worriedly:

'She hasn't got us into any trouble, I hope? The office notified me this afternoon that she has been bought out. But when I told her the good news, she seemed frightened. She wasn't glad at all!'

'Wait till you see her when we are leaving! Don't bother to go up. I'll find her room.'

He climbed the narrow staircase, and knocked on the door marked with Silver Fairy's name.

'I am ill, can't see anyone!' he heard her call out.

'Not even me?' Ma Joong shouted through the door.

It flew open and Silver Fairy pulled him inside.

'I am so glad you came!' she said eagerly, smiling through her tears. 'Something terrible has happened! You must help us, Ma Joong!'

'Us?' he asked, astonished. Then he saw Kia Yu-po sitting cross-legged on the bed. He was looking as dejected as usual. Dumbfounded, Ma Joong took the stool the girl pushed over to him. Seating herself on the bed close to the young poet, she began excitedly:

'Kia Yu-po wanted to marry me but he had lost all his money, and then that awful Miss Feng got her hooks into him!

He always has such terrible bad luck, the poor boy!' She gave the youngster an affectionate look. 'And tonight came the worst blow of all! Imagine, some wretched man has bought me! We had been hoping all along that we would be able to find some way out, but this is the end! You are an officer of the tribunal, aren't you? Can't you talk to the magistrate, and make him do something about this?'

Ma Joong pushed his cap back and slowly scratched his head. Giving the poet a dubious look, he asked him:

'What's all this talk about marrying? Weren't you going to the capital first, to pass the examinations to become an official of sorts?'

'Heaven forbid! That plan goes back to a weak moment of mistaken ambition. No, my ideal is to have a small house somewhere in the country, a woman that suits me, and to write poetry. You don't think I would ever make a good official, do you?'

'No!' Ma Joong said with conviction.

'Exactly what your boss gave me to understand! Well, there you are. If only I had the money, I would have bought this fine girl out and settled down with her in some small place. We'd be satisfied if we had enough for our daily bowl of rice, and a small jug of wine now and then. And the money for that I can always earn by becoming a schoolmaster.'

'A schoolmaster!' Ma Joong exclaimed with a shudder.

'He is wonderful as a teacher!' Silver Fairy said proudly. 'He explained a very difficult poem to me. He is so patient!'

Ma Joong gave the pair a thoughtful look.

'Well,' he said slowly, 'suppose now that I could arrange something for you two. Will you, Mr Poet, promise to take this girl back to her native village and marry her properly there?'

'Of course! But what are you talking about, my friend? Only this afternoon you advised me to marry Miss Feng, then to . . .'

'Ha!' Ma Joong shouted hastily. 'I was only testing you then, young man! We officers of the tribunal, we are deep fellows, I tell you! We always know more than you'd think! Of course I knew all along about you and this wench—tested her too, in a manner of speaking. Now then, I was very lucky at the tables here. Since she is from my own village and since she likes you, I decided this afternoon to buy her out for you.' He pulled the receipts from his sleeve and gave them to Silver Fairy. Then he took the red package with the silver and threw that to the youngster. 'And here are travelling funds and something to get yourself started as a schoolmaster. Don't say no, you fool, there's plenty more where that came from! Good luck!'

He got up and quickly left.

When he was down in the hall, Silver Fairy came running after him.

'Ma Joong!' she panted. 'You are wonderful! May I call you elder brother?'

'Always!' he said jovially. Then he frowned and added: 'By the way, my boss the judge is interested in your young man. I don't think it's anything serious, but don't leave the island until noon tomorrow. If you haven't heard from me before then, you can start travelling!'

As he opened the door she quickly stepped up close to him, and said:

'I am so glad that you knew all the time about Kia and me! When you came in just now I was just a little bit worried, elder brother. For when you . . . tested me over at the Widow Wang's, I really thought for a moment that you might have fallen in love with me, you know!'

Ma Joong guffawed.

'Don't give yourself ideas, little sister! Fact is that when I do a thing, I like to do it proper, putting in all the trimmings, so to speak!'

'You naughty rascal!' she said, pouting.

He slapped her behind and walked off.

Sauntering down the street he found to his astonishment that he really didn't know whether he was glad or sad. He shook his sleeves and found them very light; he discovered that he had only a few coppers left. Not enough for any of the varied pleasures offered by Paradise Island. He thought about taking a good walk in the park, but his head felt heavy. Better go to bed early. He entered the first doss-house he saw, and invested his coppers in one night's lodging.

He stepped out of his boots, loosened his sash and stretched himself out on his back on the common plank-bed, between two snoring loafers. His head on his folded hands, he stared up at the cracked ceiling, covered with cobwebs.

It struck him that he had a queer way of spending his nights on the gay Paradise Island. First on the floor of an attic, then on a plank-bed at five coppers. 'Must have been that confounded Soul-changing Bridge I crossed coming here!' he muttered. Then he resolutely closed his eyes and told himself sternly:

'Go to sleep . . . elder brother!'

# XVIII

After Judge Dee had drunk several cups of tea, the old clerk came in and announced that the warden's palankeen had arrived in the front courtyard. The judge rose and went to meet Feng and Jade Ring in the corridor.

'My apologies for disturbing you so late in the night!' he addressed his visitors briskly. 'Again new facts have been brought to my attention. I trust that a discussion thereof will considerably simplify our pending problems.'

He led them into the sitting-room and insisted that also Jade Ring take a seat at the table. Feng Dai's face was as inscrutable as ever, but there was anxiety in his daughter's large eyes. Judge Dee himself poured out tea for the guests, then he asked Feng:

'Did you hear that this afternoon two of your men were attacked by a band of ruffians?'

'I did, sir. The attack was organized by hooligans from over the river, to avenge three of their gang who had been killed by my special constables during a recent hold-up. I deeply regret that Your Honour's lieutenant was attacked too.'

'He doesn't mind, he is accustomed to such frays. Likes them even.' Turning to the girl, he asked: 'Could you tell me, just to put the record straight, how you entered this room the other night?'

She cast a quick look at the closed veranda door.

'I'll show you,' she said rising.

The judge got up and took her arm as she made for the door. He said:

'Don't bother! Since you came through the park, you went up on the veranda by the broad steps in the middle, I suppose?'

'Yes.' Then she bit her lips as she saw that her father's face had suddenly grown pale.

'Just as I had thought!' Judge Dee said sternly. 'Let's stop this comedy, shall we? The only steps the veranda has are at the right and left ends. You were never here, young girl. This afternoon, when I started questioning your father, you took your cue from my opening remarks about the Academician desiring you, and your father having been seen here on the night of his death. You are very clever, you made up a tale on the spot about his trying to rape you here and your killing him—all because you thought that the story would save your father.' Seeing that the red-faced girl was on the verge of tears, he continued in a more gentle voice: 'Your story was partly true, of course. The Academician did indeed make an attempt at raping you. But not three days ago, and not here in this sitting-room. It all happened ten days ago, and on board the boat. The bruises you so obligingly showed me had become discoloured; they could hardly have been of such recent origin. Your description of your struggle with the man wasn't very convincing either. If a strong man sees the girl he is assaulting grabbing a dagger, he'll of course try to wrest that weapon from her and not go on embracing her, dagger and all. And you forgot also that it was the right jugular vein that was cut. That points to suicide rather than to murder. But, apart from those slips, you made up a nice story, I must say!'

Jade Ring burst out in sobs. Feng gave her a worried look, then he said in a tired voice:

'It's all my fault, Your Honour. She was only trying to help me. When you seemed to believe her story, I couldn't bring up the courage to tell you the truth. I didn't kill that wretched Academician, but I realize that I'll have to stand trial for his murder. For I was indeed in the Red Pavilion that night. I . . .'

'No,' the judge interrupted, 'you won't be tried for murdering him. I have proof that the Academician did indeed commit suicide. Your interfering with the dead body served to emphasize the fact that he had killed himself. I presume that you came here that night in order to ask him for an explanation of his plotting against you, together with the curio-dealer?'

'Yes, Your Honour. My men had reported to me that Wen Yuan would have a box containing a large amount of money smuggled into my house. Then the Academician would warn the provincial authorities that I was submitting wrong tax-declarations. When I denied it, the money would be "found" in my house. Since, in my opinion . . .'

'Why didn't you report that plot to me at once?' Judge Dee asked curtly.

Feng looked embarrassed. After some hesitation, he answered:

'We of this island hang very much together, sir. It has always been our custom to settle ourselves all quarrels among us, we find it . . . awkward to bother people from outside with our local feuds. Perhaps it is wrong, but we . . .'

'It certainly is wrong!' the judge interrupted peevishly. 'Proceed with your story!'

'When my men had reported Wen Yuan's scheming against me, Your Honour, I decided to go and see the Academician. I wanted to ask him openly what he, the son of an eminent man whom I had known well, meant by taking part in a sordid plot against me. At the same time I wanted to take him to task about his trying to assault my daughter, on the boat. However, on my way here I met Wen Yuan, in the park. It was very strange, somehow or other this meeting reminded me of that other night, thirty years ago, when I had met Wen on my way here to see Tao Kwang. I told Wen that his treacherous plans were known to me, and that I was going to see the Academician about it. Wen Yuan was profuse in his apologies, he admitted that he had in a weak moment discussed with the

Academician a plan to oust me from my position. Since the Academician was apparently in urgent need of money, he had at first agreed. But then he had, for some reason or other, reconsidered and told Wen that the plan was off. Wen urged me to go on and talk with the Academician, he would bear him out.

'When I entered this room, I knew that my vague foreboding had been right. The Academician was sitting here slumped in his chair, dead. Had Wen known about this, and intended me to be discovered with the dead body, to accuse me of having murdered him? Thirty years ago I had suspected Wen of a similar scheme, namely to have me accused of murdering Tao Kwang. Then I remembered how that old murder had been staged as a suicide, and decided to apply the same trick. The rest was exactly as I told Your Honour this afternoon. When it had been established that the Academician had killed himself because of his unrequited love for Autumn Moon, I told my daughter everything. That made her decide on her impulsive attempt at covering up my tampering with the body.' He cleared his throat and resumed unhappily: 'Words don't suffice to express how sorry I am about all this, Your Honour. Never in my life did I feel so ashamed of myself as when I had to support Your Honour's mistaken interpretation of the Academician's last scribblings. I really . . .'

'I don't mind being made a fool of,' Judge Dee remarked dryly. 'I am accustomed to it, it's happening to me all the time. Fortunately I usually discover it before it's too late, though. Well, as a matter of fact the Academician's last scribblings did refer to Autumn Moon. But he didn't kill himself because of her.' The judge leaned back in his chair. Stroking his long black beard, he went on slowly: 'The Academician was a man of great talent, but of a cold and calculating nature. His success came too soon, it went to his head. He had become an Academician, now he wanted to rise higher still, and quickly. But for that he needed much money, and he didn't have that, for the family estate had declined through bad harvests and reckless speculation. Therefore he worked out, together with your old enemy Wen Yuan, a plan to get access to the fabulous wealth of Paradise Island. Ten days ago he arrived here to execute that plan, confident and overbearing. When he saw your daughter that night on the boat, his stupid pride was hurt by her refusal, and he tried to rape her. When the curio-dealer came to meet him on the landing stage, he was still chafing under that rebuff, and ordered Wen to help him to get your daughter, reminding him that soon you would be arrested and sent to the capital, found guilty of tax-evasion. Wen then took heart and suggested how he could force your daughter to grant him her favours. That rascally curio-dealer saw there his chance to deal you also a personal blow.'

Judge Dee took a sip from his tea. He resumed:

'However, after his arrival here the Academician got so busy amusing himself with Carnation, Peony and other beautiful courtesans that he forgot all about your daughter. But not about the plan to oust you. He met at the gaming table a young man whom he thought he might use for concealing the money in your mansion.

'Then, on the 25th, the day of his death, the Academician made a discovery, or thought he had made a discovery, that changed everything for him. He paid off the three courtesans he had been sleeping with, and he sent his sponging booncompanions home, back to the capital. For he had decided to put an end to his own life. In the evening, before executing this plan, he walked over to the pavilion of the Queen Flower, for a last meeting with her.

'Since they are both dead, we shall never know what their exact relationship was. According to what I heard, however, the Academician invited her to his parties just to lend glamour to them, he never got round to trying to sleep with her. And perhaps for that very reason she became to him, in his last hours, the symbol of all the earthly pleasures he was about to renounce. In that nostalgic mood he entrusted her with a letter to his father, which she forgot to deliver. She had not tried to make him her lover, probably because her intuition had told her that he had the same cold, utterly selfish character as she herself. And he certainly never offered to redeem her.'

'Never wanted to buy her out? But that's preposterous, sir!' Feng exclaimed. 'She said so herself!'

'She did. But that was a lie. When she heard that he had killed himself, and left a few scribblings referring to her, she thought that an excellent chance to bolster further her reputation in the world of the "flowers and willows". She boldly stated that she had refused the flattering offer of this famous young scholar.'

'She offended against the unwritten code of elegant life!' Feng burst out angrily. 'Her name shall be struck from the list of Queen Flowers.'

'She wasn't better than she should have been,' Judge Dee remarked dryly, 'but it was your trade that made her so. Another reason for not speaking harshly of her is that she died a most horrible death.'

The judge cast a quick glance at the closed veranda door. He passed his hand over his face. Then he fixed his two visitors with his penetrating eyes and resumed:

'You, Feng, tampered with the evidence of a suicide. And you, Jade Ring, told me a string of lies. However, fortunately for you, you two lied to me in informal conversation, you didn't put your false testimony in writing, marked with your seal and thumbprint. Neither do I forget that when you, Feng, swore to me that you were telling me the complete truth, you said emphatically that this oath was limited to your account of what happened thirty years ago. Well, the law defines the ultimate aim of justice as redressing, as much as possible, the damage wrought by a crime. And attempted rape is a crime, and a very serious one too. Therefore I shall forget about the mistakes you and your daughter made, and I shall have the Academician's suicide now registered as such, including the alleged motive of unrequited love. There is no sense in spoiling the reputation the unfortunate Queen Flower left here, so you shan't mention her deceit, and you shan't strike her name from the list.

'As regards the curio-dealer Wen Yuan, he is guilty of malicious plotting. But he did that in such an ineffectual way that all his clumsy plans came to nought before he had even dared to begin their execution. He probably never committed any real crime, his character is mean enough but he lacks the courage to translate his cowardly, underhanded schemings into action. I shall take appropriate measures for preventing Wen, once and for all, from getting up schemes against you, and from maltreating defenceless girls.

'Two capital crimes were committed here in the Red Pavilion. Since, however, neither you nor your daughter, nor, indeed, Wen Yuan, had any part in them, I shan't discuss those dark deeds. That's all I have to say to you.'

Feng rose and knelt in front of Judge Dee, and his daughter followed his example. They started to protest their gratitude for his leniency but the judge cut them short impatiently. He made them rise, and said:

'I disapprove of Paradise Island, Feng, and of all that goes on here. But I do realize that in a way such resorts are a necessary evil. And a good warden like you ensures that it is at least a controlled evil. You can go.'

When Feng was taking his leave he asked, somewhat diffidently:

'I suppose it would be presumptuous to ask you, sir, what two capital crimes Your Honour was referring to just now?'

The judge considered this question for a while. Then he replied:

'Not presumptuous, no. After all, you are the warden here, you have a right to know. Premature, rather. For my theory has not yet been confirmed. As soon as I have obtained that confirmation, I shall let you know.'

Feng and his daughter made their obeisance and left.

## XIX

The next morning Ma Joong came to report for duty very early, when Judge Dee was still eating his morning rice, out on the veranda. A thin mist hung over the silent park; the wet garlands of coloured silk drooped limply among the trees.

The judge gave his lieutenant a brief account of his talk with Feng and his daughter. He concluded: 'Presently we shall go and try to find Miss Ling. Tell the manager to have two horses ready for us. If Miss Ling is not back in her hovel, we'll have to make a fairly long ride up-country, to the north of the island.'

When Ma Joong came back Judge Dee was just putting down his chopsticks. He rose and went inside, telling Ma Joong to lay out his brown travelling robe. While helping the judge to change, Ma asked:

'I suppose that Kia Yu-po isn't implicated in all those queer goings on, sir?'

'No. Why?'

'I happened to hear last night that he plans to leave the island, together with a girl he has fallen in love with. His engagement to Miss Feng was more or less foisted on him, I gathered.'

'Let them go. I don't need him. I think we'll be able to leave here too today, Ma Joong. In your spare hours you got all the amusement you wanted, I trust?'

'I did indeed! But Paradise Island is a very expensive place!'

'I don't doubt it,' the judge said, winding the black sash round his waist. 'But you had two silver pieces, those'll have sufficed.'

'To tell you the truth, sir, they didn't! I had a very good time, but all my money is gone.'

'Well, I hope it was worth it! And you still have your capital, the gold you inherited from your uncle.'

'That's gone too, sir,' Ma Joong remarked.

'What's that? Those two gold bars you intended to save for later? That's incredible!'

Ma Joong nodded sadly.

'The fact is, Your Honour, that I found here too many attractive girls, far too many! And far too expensive!'

'It's disgraceful!' Judge Dee burst out. 'Squandering two whole gold bars on wine and women!' He adjusted his black cap with an angry jerk. Then he sighed and said with a resigned shrug: 'You'll never learn, Ma Joong.'

They walked in silence to the front courtyard and ascended their horses.

Riding ahead, Ma Joong took the judge through the back streets and across the piece of wasteland. At the entrance of the path leading on among the trees, he halted his horse and remarked that it was there that he and his two friends had been attacked. He asked:

'Did Feng know what was behind that attack, sir?'

'He thinks he does, but he doesn't. I know. It was aimed at me.'

Ma Joong wanted to asked what that meant but the judge had already urged on his horse. When the large yew-tree came into sight Ma Joong pointed at the hovel standing against its gnarled trunk. Judge Dee nodded. He dismounted and handed the reins of his horse to Ma Joong, saying:

'You stay here and wait for me.'

He walked on alone through the wet grass. The morning sun had not yet succeeded in piercing the dense foliage that overhung the shed's roof. It was clammy in the shadow; there was an unpleasant odour of rotting leaves. A faint shimmer of light appeared behind the dirty oil-paper of the single window.

Judge Dee stepped up close to the ramshackle door and listened. He heard a strangely beautiful voice softly croon an

162

old melody. He remembered that it had been popular when he was still a child. He pulled the door open and entered. While he was standing there, just inside the entrance, the door fell shut behind him, creaking on rusty hinges.

The light of a cheap earthenware oil lamp lit the drab room with its uncertain light. Miss Ling was sitting cross-legged on the bamboo couch, cradling the repulsive head of the leprous beggar in her arms. He was lying flat on his back on the couch, the sores on his limbs showed through the soiled rags that partly covered his emaciated body. His one remaining eye shone dully in the lamp-light.

She raised her head and turned her blind face to the judge.

'Who is it?' she asked in her rich, warm voice.

'It is I, the magistrate.'

The leper's blue lips contorted in a lopsided sneer. Looking fixedly at his one eye, the judge spoke:

'You are Dr Lee Wei-djing, the Academician's father. And she is the courtesan Green Jade, reported dead thirty years ago.'

'We are lovers!' the blind woman said proudly.

'You came to the island,' Judge Dee continued to the leper, 'because you had heard that the Queen Flower Autumn Moon had driven your son to his death, and you wanted revenge. You were wrong. Your son killed himself because he had discovered swellings, on his neck, and thought that he had got the disease too. Whether rightly or wrongly, I don't know; I couldn't examine the corpse. He lacked your courage, he couldn't face a leper's miserable end. But Autumn Moon didn't know that. In her foolish hankering after fame she stated that he had killed himself because of her. You heard that from her own lips when, hidden in the shrubbery in front of the veranda of the Red Pavilion, you eavesdropped on our conversation.'

He paused. There was only the laboured breathing of the leper.

'Your son trusted Autumn Moon. He gave her a letter for you wherein he explained his decision. But she forgot all about

163

it, didn't even open it. I found it, after you had murdered her.'

He took the letter from his sleeve, and read it aloud.

'I bore a son of you under my heart, dear,' the woman said tenderly. 'But after I was cured, I had a miscarriage. Our son would have been handsome, and courageous. Just like you!'

Judge Dee threw the letter on the couch.

'After you had come to the island you were watching Autumn Moon all the time. When, late that night, you saw her going to the Red Pavilion, you went after her. Standing on the veranda you saw her through the barred window, lying naked on the bed. You called her name. Then you stood yourself next to the window, your back against the wall. When she came to the window, probably pressing her face close to the iron bars to see better who was calling, you suddenly came forward. You stuck your hands through the bars and grabbed her throat, to throttle her. But your deformed hands could not hold her. On her way to the door to call for help, she had a heart attack and collapsed on the floor. You killed her, Dr Lee.'

The red, inflamed eyelid fluttered. She bent over the deformed face and whispered:

'Don't listen to him, dear! Rest, my sweet, you are not well.'

The judge averted his eyes. Staring at the damp floor of stamped earth, he went on:

'Your son rightly mentioned in his letter your indomitable courage, Dr Lee. You were mortally ill and your wealth had dwindled away. But you still had your son. You would make him a great man, and quickly too. Paradise Island, that treasure house of gold, was situated on the boundary of your land. First you sent your ruffians to rob Feng's gold transport, but it was too well guarded. Then you thought of a better plan. You told your son that the curio-dealer Wen Yuan hated Feng and wanted to oust him as warden. You ordered your son to establish contact with Wen, and execute with him the plot that would result in Feng's being dismissed in disgrace. Your son would then get Wen appointed in Feng's place as warden of the

164

island, and through him you would be able to tap the island's wealth. Your son's death brought all that to nought.

'We hadn't met before, Dr Lee, but you knew my reputation, just as I knew yours, and you were afraid I would find out about you. After you had killed the Queen Flower, you came back to the Red Pavilion. You stood for a while on the veranda watching me through the barred window. Your evil presence only caused me a bad dream. You couldn't do anything, for I was lying too far from the window, and I had barred the door.'

He looked up. The leper's face was a gruesome, leering mask. The putrid odour in the small room had become worse. The judge pulled up his neckcloth over his mouth and nose and spoke through it:

'You tried to leave the island after that, but the boatmen wouldn't take you. I suppose you searched the forest on the waterside for a hiding place, and there met by accident, after thirty years, your mistress Green Jade. Recognized her by her voice, I presume. She warned you that I was investigating Tao Kwang's death. What made you cling to a life that held only misery for you, Dr Lee? Were you determined to save your reputation at any cost? Or was it devotion to the woman whom you loved, thirty years ago, and whom you had thought dead? Or an evil desire to come out winner, always? I don't know how an incurable disease may affect a great mind.' As there was no reply, Judge Dee resumed: 'Yesterday afternoon you spied again on me, for the third time. I should have known, I should have recognized the unmistakable odour. You heard me saying to my lieutenant that I was going here. You went to call your hired men and ordered them to lie in ambush among the trees and kill me. You could not know that, after I had gone inside the sitting-room, I had changed my plans. Your men attacked my lieutenant and two of the warden's men instead. All were killed, but one of them mentioned your name, just before he died.

'After I had read your son's letter, I suddenly understood. I knew what you had been, Dr Lee. Feng had described you as the dashing young official of thirty years ago. And Green Jade described you again when she spoke to me of a lover with a wild, reckless strain in him, a man who would casually throw away wealth, position, everything—because of the woman he loved.'

'That was you, dear!' the woman spoke softly. 'That was you, my handsome, reckless lover!'

She covered his face with kisses.

Judge Dee looked away. He said in a tired voice:

'Persons suffering from an incurable disease are beyond the pale of the law, Dr Lee. I only wish to state that you murdered the courtesan Autumn Moon in the Red Pavilion, as you murdered there Tao Kwang, thirty years ago.'

'Thirty years!' the beautiful voice spoke up. 'After all those years we are together again! Those years never happened, dear, they were a bad dream, a nightmare. It was only yesterday that we met, in the Red Room . . . red as our passion, our burning, reckless love. Nobody ever knew we met there, you, the handsome, talented young official, loving me, the most beautiful, the most talented of all courtesans, the Queen Flower of Paradise Island! Feng Dai, Tao Kwang, and so many others, they all sought my favour. I encouraged them, feigned not to be able to make up my mind, only to protect our secret, our sweet secret.

'Then came that last evening . . . when was it? Wasn't it last night? Just when you were crushing my trembling body in your strong arms, we suddenly heard someone in the sitting-room. You sprang from the bed, naked as you were you ran out there. I followed you, saw you standing there, the red rays of the setting sun colouring your dear body a fiery red. When Tao Kwang saw us standing there close together, naked and defiant, he grew white with rage. Pulling his dagger he called me a shameful name. "Kill him!" I cried. You sprang on him, wrenched the dagger from his hand and plunged it into his neck. The blood spouted over you, red blood over your red, broad breast. Never, never have I loved you more than then . . .'

The ecstatic joy gave the ravaged blind face a strange beauty. The judge bent his head. He heard the vibrant voice resume:

'I said: "Let's dress quickly and flee!" We went back to the Red Room, but then heard someone enter the sitting-room. You went and saw that silly boy. He rushed out again at once, but you said that he might recognize you. It was better to take the body to the Red Room, put the dagger in his hand, lock the door behind us, push the key back inside under the door . . . then they'd say that Tao had killed himself.

'We parted on the veranda. They were just lighting the lampions, in the small kiosk, over in the park. You said you would go away for a few weeks, wait till the suicide had been registered. Then . . . you would come back to me.'

She began to cough. It became steadily worse, soon it was shaking her wasted frame. Foam and blood came on her lips. She wiped it off carelessly and went on, her voice suddenly weak and hoarse:

'They asked me whether Tao had loved me. I said yes he had loved me, and it was true. They asked me whether he had died because I would not have him, and I said yes he had died because of me, for again it was true. But then the sickness came. . . . I got it, my face, my hands . . . my eyes. I would die, and I wanted to die, die rather than ever let you see me again, as I had become. . . . There was the fire, other sick women dragged me along, over the bridge, to the forest.

'I didn't die, I lived. I, who wanted to die! I took the papers of Miss Ling, Gold Jasper as she was called. She had died, in the field drain, by my side. I came back, but you thought I was dead, as I wanted you to think. How glad I was when I heard how great, how famous you had become! It was the only

167

thing that kept me alive. And now, at last, you have come back to me, in my arms!'

Suddenly the voice fell silent. When Judge Dee looked up he saw her thin, spidery fingers quickly passing over the still head in her lap. The one eye had closed, the rags on the sunken breast did not move any more.

Pressing the ugly head to her flat bosom she cried out:

'You came back, Heaven be praised! You came back so that you could die in my arms . . . and I with you.'

She hugged the dead body, whispering endearing words.

The judge turned round and went outside. The creaking door fell shut behind him.

# XX

When Judge Dee had rejoined Ma Joong, his lieutenant asked eagerly:

'You were quite some time. What did she say, sir?'

The judge wiped the beads of perspiration from his forehead, then swung himself on his horse. He muttered:

'No one was there.' Taking a deep breath of the fresh morning air, he added: 'I made a thorough search of her lodging, but found nothing. I had a theory, but it proved to be wrong. Let's ride back to our hostel.'

While they were crossing the piece of waste land, Ma Joong suddenly pointed ahead with his riding-whip and exclaimed:

'Look at all that smoke over there, sir! They have begun to burn the altars. The Festival of the Dead is over!'

The judge stared at the dense columns of black smoke billowing over the rooftops.

'Yes,' he said, 'the Gates of the Other World have closed.' Closed, he thought, on the ghosts of the past. Thirty years the shadows of that one night in the Red Pavilion had dragged on, darkening the lives of the living. And now at last, after thirty long years, those shadows had slunk away to that dank, evil-smelling hovel; now they were cowering there, with a dead man, and a dying woman. Soon they would have gone, gone for ever, never to come back.

When they had returned to the Hostel of Eternal Bliss, Judge Dee told the manager to prepare the bill. He ordered the groom to look after the horses, then went on with Ma Joong to the Red Pavilion.

While Ma Joong was packing the saddlebags, the judge sat down and re-read his report on the Academician's suicide that he had drawn up the night before, then wrote the concluding passage of his report on the demise of Autumn Moon. He gave as his verdict that she had died from a heart attack, after over-indulgence in alcohol.

Afterwards he wrote a brief letter to Feng Dai, stating that he had found that one and the same man had murdered both Tao Kwang and Autumn Moon, but that the criminal had died and that these matters therefore would be best let alone. In conclusion he wrote: 'I am informed that Dr Lee Wei-djing, his mind deranged by the last phase of leprosy, has been roaming about in this area, and died in the hovel of the former courtesan Miss Ling, who is mortally ill. Should the woman have died also, I order you to have the hovel burned, together with the two corpses, so as to prevent the disease from spreading. Inform the Lee family. The woman has no known relatives.' Then he signed the letter. Having re-read it he again moistened his writing brush and added a postscript, saying: 'I also learned that Kia Yu-po has left the island together with a girl he loves. An older and deeper affection shall comfort your daughter, to whom convey my best wishes for her future happiness.'

He took a new sheet and indited a letter to Tao Pan-te, informing him that his father's murderer had been identified, but that he had died after a long and painful disease. He added: 'Thus Heaven has avenged your wrong, and nothing stands in the way of a closer union between the houses of Tao and Feng, sealing the old friendship.'

He closed the two letters and marked them 'personal'. Then he rolled up his official reports, together with all the enclosures, and put the bulky roll in his sleeve. Getting up from his chair, he said to Ma Joong:

'We'll go home via Chin-hwa. There I'll hand my report to Magistrate Lo.'

They walked to the hall together, Ma Joong carrying the saddlebags.

Judge Dee settled the bill with the manager, and handed

him the letters to Feng Dai and Tao Pan-te, for immediate delivery.

Just as they had stepped out into the front courtyard to mount their horses, there was a clanging of gongs in the street outside, and loud shouts of 'Make way, make way!'

A dozen perspiring bearers carried a large official palankeen inside. It was followed by a troop of constables, holding high the large red placards inscribed with Magistrate Lo's full rank and titles. Their headman moved the door curtain aside with a respectful bow, and Magistrate Lo descended, resplendent in his green official robe and winged judge's cap, and vigorously fanning himself with a small folding fan.

When he saw Judge Dee standing by his horse he ran up to him with mincing steps, exclaiming excitedly:

'My dear Elder Brother, what a terrible thing! The Queen Flower of Paradise Island dead, and under mysterious circumstances! The whole province'll be talking about it! Came rushing back here, despite this awful heat. As soon as I heard the shocking news! Wouldn't dream of saddling you with more extra work, of course!'

'Her death must indeed have been a shock to you,' the judge remarked dryly.

Lo gave him a shrewd look. He said airily:

'I am always interested in a beautiful woman, Dee, always! "Along the dusty road of weary life's routine, blooms all too rare this full-blown rose, that laves the traveller with its dew-decked sheen, and tee-tums him to sweet repose"—that's how I put it in a recent poem. I am still groping for a telling verb in the last line. Not bad though, eh? Well, what happened to the poor girl?'

Judge Dee handed him the roll of documents.

'It's all here, Lo. I had planned to pass by Chin-hwa to hand you these papers, but you'll allow me to give them to you here and now. I am eager to get home.'

'By all means!' Lo closed his fan and stuck it jauntily in

his collar behind his head. Then he quickly unrolled the papers. When he had glanced the first report through he nodded and said:

'I see you confirmed my verdict of the Academician's suicide. Mere matter of routine. As I told you.'

He went on with the report on the Queen Flower's death. After he had verified that his own name was not mentioned in connection with her he nodded approvingly, rolled all the documents up and said with a contented smile:

'Excellent work, Dee! Ably written too. I can send the report on to the Prefect unchanged—practically unchanged, that is. Style seems a bit on the heavy side, if I may say so, Dee. I'll give it a somewhat lighter touch here and there, make it easier to read. Modern style, that's what the metropolitan officials like nowadays, you know. I am told you can even put in a bit of humour—very subdued, needless to say. Shan't fail to mention your valuable assistance, of course.' Putting the papers in his sleeve, he asked briskly: 'Well, who caused the Queen Flower's death? You have locked him up in the warden's place, I suppose?'

'When you have read the rest of my report,' Judge Dee replied evenly, 'you'll perceive that the Queen Flower died of a heart attack.'

'But everybody is saying that you refused to confirm the coroner's verdict! The Mystery of the Red Pavilion, they call it. Almighty Heaven, Dee, you don't mean to say that I'll have to continue the investigation?'

'It's indeed something of a mystery. But my verdict of accidental death is amply supported by proof. You can rest assured that the higher authorities will consider the case closed.'

Lo sighed with undisguised relief.

'There's only one thing left to do,' Judge Dee continued. 'Among the papers you'll find a confession of the curio-dealer Wen Yuan. He delivered false testimony in court and tortured a courtesan. He deserves a flogging, but that would probably kill him. I propose that you have him stand in the pillory a day, with a notice stating that he is under a suspended sentence, and that he'll be flogged as soon as a new complaint is lodged against him.'

'I'll do that with pleasure! The scoundrel has fine porcelain, but his prices are atrocious. He'll bring them down a bit now, I presume. Well, I am deeply obliged, Dee. Sorry to see you are leaving already. I may as well stay on a bit here to ah . . . study the aftermath of the cases. Have you seen yet the new dancer that arrived here yesterday? No? They say she is absolutely wonderful, remarkable skill, and a charming voice too. And a figure . . .' With a pensive smile he twirled his moustache, elegantly lifting his little finger. Suddenly he gave the judge a searching look. Raising his eyebrows, he added loftily: 'I am disappointed, though, that you didn't get to the bottom of that mystery of the Red Pavilion. Dee. Heavens, man, you have the reputation of being the most clever judge of our whole province! Always thought you solved murders and things in between two cups of tea, so to speak!'

'Reputations are not always founded on fact!' the judge remarked with a bleak smile. 'I'll be off now, back to Poo-yang. Do come and see me next time you call there. Goodbye!'

# POSTSCRIPT

JUDGE DEE was a historical person; he lived from 630 to 700 A.D., during the Tang dynasty. Besides earning fame as a great detective, he was also a brilliant statesman who, in the second half of his career, played an important role in the internal and foreign policies of the Tang Empire. The adventures related here, however, are entirely fictitious, although many features were suggested to me by original old Chinese sources.

A good description of Judge Dee's later life will be found in chapters 37-41 of Lin Yutang's book *Lady Wu: A True Story*, published by Heinemann in 1957. There his name is transcribed Di Renjiay.

The plates I drew in the style of sixteenth century Chinese illustrated blockprints, and they represent, therefore, costumes and customs of the Ming period rather than those of the Tang dynasty. Note that in Judge Dee's time the Chinese did not wear pigtails; that custom was imposed on them after 1644 A.D. when the Manchus had conquered China. The men did their hair up in a top-knot, they wore caps both inside and outside the house. They did not smoke; tobacco and opium were introduced into China only many centuries later.

i-iii-1961

ROBERT VAN GULIK